PIERCE MacKENZIE

A SIGNET BOOK
NEW AMERICAN LIBRARY

NAL BOOKS ARE AVAILABLE AT QUANTITY DISCOUNTS WHEN USED TO PROMOTE PRODUCTS OR SERVICES. FOR INFORMATION PLEASE WRITE TO PREMIUM MARKETING DIVISION, NEW AMERICAN LIBRARY, 1633 BROADWAY, NEW YORK, NEW YORK 10019.

SIGNET TRADEMARK REG. U.S. PAT. OFF. AND FOREIGN COUNTRIES
REGISTERED TRADEMARK—MARCA REGISTRADA
HECHO EN CHICAGO, U.S.A.

SIGNET, SIGNET CLASSIC, MENTOR, ONYX, PLUME, MERIDIAN and NAL BOOKS are published by New American Library, 1633 Broadway, New York, New York 10019

First Printing, February, 1987

1 2 3 4 5 6 7 8 9

PRINTED IN THE UNITED STATES OF AMERICA

TWO-TIMING WOMEN

T.G. Horne figured there was something funny about the girl when she told him her name was Gertrude, when before she had called herself Gilda. Then she asked his name, though he had already told her it. She was hiding something, but when she lifted her silk negligée over her head, what she *wasn't* hiding interested him too much to care.

In fact, he stopped caring about anything except what he was doing—until the door swung open. There stood the girl he was in bed with. Her—or her identical twin.

"I told you ten o'clock," said Gertrude from the bed.

"I came early. Hope I'm not too late," said Gilda, unbuttoning her dress as she moved into the room.

T.G. Horne was in double trouble—but he figured he might just be able to handle it. . . .

1

The discovery of gold or silver in one's back yard can turn out to be a mixed blessing. For you and for the yard. The epidemic of silver strikes around Fodder City, Wyoming, proved a case in point. Overnight the community earned the fanciful epithet "the wealthiest metropolis in Wyoming Territory." Unfortunately, the discoveries attracted a troupe of adventuresome rabble, con and quick-dollar artists, gamesters from far and wide, among them Eleanor Dumont (Madame Moustache), Ed "Dirty Face" Jones, Riley Grannan, and the notorious Col. Charles Norton.

But Fodder City was not to sink into iniquity without a fight. Also arriving in town was a gentleman in his early seventies, his head crowned with a magnificent mane of snow-white hair, his face distinguished by piercing blue eyes and a patrician nose, his voice deep, melodious, and capable of mesmerizing multitudes, his manner cultured and refined. Bishop Bolton Winfield came of his own volition, perceiving from afar that danger threatened, but that it could be averted by the combined efforts of the honest, hardworking, god-fearing people of the community. Bishop Winfield called together Fodder City's five clergymen for what he described as a council of war against the insidious element that sought to prey on the miners and townspeople.

The meeting was held in the office of the Rev. Cletus O. Miller of the Congregational church. Present with Rev. Miller were Father Patrick Dunphy of St. Mary's church, Rev. Ewart D. Hollings of the Presbyterian church, Amos Grier, the local Methodist shepherd, and Rev. Hildreth Lacklund of the Baptist church.

"These ne'er-do-wells have invaded us like a swarm of locusts," lamented Rev. Grier. "They've even approached me with donations. I refused to accept a thin dime, of course. I'll not help them salve their consciences."

Father Dunphy sighed. "What's so grim is the prospect of seeing so much wealth siphoned into their pockets, money that could be doing the community great good, improving, uplifting . . ."

"Quite right, Patrick," said Rev. Miller. "So much is needed here. What can we do to protect our flocks and ourselves from these parasites? They won't let up until they've turned Fodder City into Gomorrah."

Rev. Lacklund and Rev. Hollings agreed. All five appeared woefully discouraged, helpless prey to pessimism. Lacklund had it that Fodder City was doomed and in six weeks would be reduced to a ghost town by the invaders' depredations.

Rev. Hollings groaned aloud. "Our hands are tied. All we can do is stand by and watch everything we've worked so hard to build come tumbling down."

"Gentlemen, gentlemen," purred Bishop Winfield, "you all sound as if you're giving up before the battle starts. Better you make a stand and fight, take on these miscreants and beat them at their own game. Isaiah, Chapter Seven, Verse Fifteen: 'Butter and honey shall he eat, that he may know how to refuse the evil, and choose the good.' "

"I don't follow you, Bishop," said Rev. Miller.

"The proud resident of this fair city, my dear fellow; we must encourage him to refuse the evil and choose the good. We must offer him an alternative. I ask you, what is your strongest weapon? Religion, of course. Your sword and your armor, and your church your mighty fortress. I personally have no prejudice against abundant wealth; what's important is what use it's put to. In this case, it either helps to accomplish good works or lines the pockets of evil men. I say we go on the attack, steal a march on these avaricious trespassers."

"How?" chorused all.

"Divert the flow into a project designed to benefit all. From the little I've seen, there's not a church in town that doesn't need improvements. Let that be your end, and the means, a lottery."

"Gambling!" Rev. Miller's eyebrows clashed above the bridge of his nose in a disapproving frown. Rev. Lacklund and Rev. Grier reacted similarly.

"We'd be playing right into the gamblers' hands," said Father Dunphy.

"Please let me finish. Yes, a lottery, the proceeds to go directly to the churches. As I came into town yesterday, I couldn't help but notice that this church badly needs a new roof."

"True, true," said Rev. Miller. "We've been trying to raise the money for nearly two years. Meanwhile, the shingles rot away and the leaks get bigger."

"Just one example," said the bishop. "I'm sure there are dozens. Gentlemen, gentlemen, there isn't one of us who doesn't take a dim view of gaming and wagering; they've been man's folly and his downfall since before Christ and Caesar. Cards and dice alone provide a hundred pits into which the well-heeled but unwary can tumble, but a lottery, scrupulously monitored, kept as clean as a hound's tooth, with the profits channeled into good works . . . Tell us, Father Dunphy, what do you need? What can St. Mary's use?"

"Name it, sir. I need new vestments, we need a baptismal font, new missals, a new statue of the Blessed Virgin. Faith, sir, I could give you a list two feet long."

"The Methodist church is on the verge of collapse," said Amos Grier.

"Tear it down and erect a new one in its place," said the bishop. "All it takes is money, and a lottery would provide every penny. Think about it. If you don't need to replace or improve something, what about adding on to what you've got? A new Sunday school, a meeting hall, a bell, an organ . . . Best of all, you'd be diverting the money from grasping evil hands into the hands of the righteous and worthy into good works. And mark my words, when the tap is turned off, these avaricious intruders will pack up and leave, moving on to greener pastures."

"I think a lottery's a splendid idea," said Rev. Hollings.

"So do I," said Rev. Lacklund. "But how do we go about it, Bishop?"

"Leave that to me," said the bishop. "I've organized many back in Minnesota and Wisconsin. Every one hugely successful. With the proceeds of the Beloit lottery the townspeople built a new Presbyterian church of New Hampshire granite, not to mention a library for the high school."

"Granite," murmured Rev. Miller.

All five faces took on expressions of yearning, a reaction not lost on the bishop. In short order his proposal was unanimously approved. It was agreed that authorization for the Grand Lottery of Crook County be sought from the territorial legislature without delay. Tickets would be printed. Ten percent of the proceeds would go to the county authorities to fund construction of a badly needed road to nearby Sundance, the county seat; 10 percent would be earmarked for promotional expenses; and after the prizes were awarded, the remainder would be equally divided among the five denominations.

"You'll need to approach the county sheriff for a license to operate," said the bishop. "The fee is usually around a hundred dollars. You'll—"

Rev. Hollings had risen to his feet. "Bother 'you'll,' good friend, 'we'll' is the word here. It's your brainchild, you've the experience, you've attained success. Gentlemen, I hereby move we place Bishop Bolton Winfield in overall charge of the grand lottery."

"Hear, hear!" burst the others.

"Gentlemen, gentlemen, you flatter me." He gestured restraint, his palms outward. "But you forget, I'm an outsider, a stranger in your midst. Overall con . . . charge is a grave responsibility. There isn't one among you who wouldn't be a far better choice than I."

They would not allow him to go on. His objections were overruled and he was installed as grand-lottery chairman. The meeting ended with Father Dunphy's invitation to all to remove to his place for a glass of port to toast the occasion. Baptist Lacklund politely declined.

Bishop Bolton Winfield also declined, pleading weariness, declaring that he'd best go back to his hotel room to nap until dinnertime.

"My heart's not as sound as it once was, my friends. My doctor advises me to rest as often as possible during the day. Perhaps another time, Father Dunphy. By all means another time, when the golden hour arrives and the five of you divide the profits. That's the occasion to toast."

They let him go reluctantly and with congratulations and expressions of gratitude.

On the way back to the Hotel Meadowlark and his room he thought about the meeting and the outcome to which he had steered it. What in the world, he wondered, induced them to agree with him that cutting into the gamblers' take would discourage them to such an extent they would leave town? How could a lottery possibly affect their activities other than to put a crimp in their profits? The naïveté of men of the cloth never ceased to surprise him.

Still, a solvent church does imbue its members with pride and a loyalty that can only bolster their faith—thereby giving them better protection against temptation.

He rounded a corner and came within sight of the Western Union office. A beautiful and beautifully dressed young woman was coming out. She glanced his way. He tipped his hat, bowed slightly, and accorded her an expression of approval that few of his station would have the audacity to display. It startled her; she managed a self-conscious smile and moved on.

Inside the office the clerk provided him with pad and pencil.

IDLENESS IS THE DEVILS
HANDMAIDEN STOP WORK THE
JOY OF THE LORD

The clerk crinkled his bony nose, squinted at the message over his spectacles, and read it a second time. Then a third. Confusion clung to his narrow face. "Is that it?"

"That's it."

"What does it mean?"

"What does it say?"

He began reading it again.

The bishop stopped him. "Just send it to Alistair Richardson, Esquire, care of the Wheatland House Hotel, Harlowton, Montana. Mr. Richardson'll understand."

"I don't."

"You don't have to. It's not being sent to you."

"Is it a riddle? I like riddles."

The bishop dagger-eyed him. "How much?"

"Fifty-five cents." He held his pencil poised. "Name, please."

"He'll know who it's from."

The bishop paid and left him still confused, rereading the wire, moving his lips as he did so, shaking his head.

The Chicago, Burlington, and Quincy train left Bowler and meandered down territory, around the southern end of the Pryor Mountains and over the border into Wyoming. Since its inception ten minutes out of Harlowton, the poker game in the second car had been going on in spirited fashion, the four players mutually agreeing to raising the stakes time and again, and the pots growing wealthier accordingly.

T. G. Horne did not look like a professional gambler. His imported Italian silk vest did not display the customary identifying hand-painted roses and violets; his shirt was not ruffled, nor did it harbor a diamond horseshoe stickpin or any jewelry. Plain buttons not ruby-set links closed his cuffs. He did wear a custom-tailored black broadcloth suit with knee-high coat, the tails tucked neatly beneath him; his imported leather boots were fashioned of Italian leather, but his thousand-dollar Jürgensen watch, its stem set with a one-carat diamond, he kept in its pocket, unencumbered by its four-foot gold chain, which lay neatly coiled beside his .45 in his bag in the rack overhead. His pistol may have been out of reach, but he was not without protection. His four-shot Sharps .22 nestled in its shoulder holster, his Barns .50 single-ball boot pistol cooled his lower right leg, and his dagger-fitted knuckle-duster was within reach in his vest pocket.

Others in the marathon game included a wizened and wheezing little antique bundle of nervous energy whose pince-nez glasses lent him the look of a hairy frog who called himself "Judge" without bothering to attach any name to the title; a happy-go-lucky and from all appearances well-heeled tinware drummer, whose suit looked as if it had been cut from a plaid horse blanket; and a poker-faced young lady with dark, brooding eyes, a cluster of little curls high on her forehead, the rest of her hair drawn back over her ears and descending in pipe curls to her shoulders. She affected no makeup, and her dress was as frilly and feminine as one could wish for to firmly establish her sex. She introduced herself as Mrs. Duffield.

For the first few hands Horne pushed the name about in his mind, certain that it would eventually ring a bell somewhere in distant memory. Her superb control of her cards, her shrewd play, and her courage confirmed her true identity to his satisfaction. Mrs. Duffield was Mrs. Duffield indeed, but her maiden name was Alice Ivers, "Poker Alice," one of the best of the train-riding professionals. If any doubt lingered that she was who he thought she was, it promptly vanished when she politely asked the others in the game for permission to smoke and lit a cigar.

South of Frannie, less than twenty minutes into Wyoming, the train ran into a waiting horde of Sioux. Within seconds arrows began raining at the train, shattering windows, thudding into the sides of the car, sticking and quivering to rest in seats, gentlemen's hats, luggage. The passengers in the second car ducked and scrambled, screamed and bellowed, with the exception of the four poker players. The warriors' bloodcurdling screams were lost on their ears; their intimidating presence, made even more frightening by their garish warpaint, was ignored. Not so much as two words of comment on their arrival passed over the pot. All four were dyed-in-the-wool poker players and, as such, were not about to permit anything or anyone to disturb their concentration or distract them from the game.

One, then another arrow whirred over their heads, passing within an inch of the crown of the tinware drummer's curly brim derby. He did not even flinch, coolly taking the pot with two pair, aces over sixes.

Having identified Poker Alice Ivers, Horne screwed his attention to her every move. After nearly four hours of play he calculated that he was about two hundred dollars to the good. The judge was the biggest loser and the tinware drummer had to be out about a thousand, which to his credit did not seem to nettle him in the least. Alice—soft-spoken, dignified in manner, every inch the well-born lady (apart from her cigar)—was the big winner.

Horne decided it was time to make his move. Happily, the train was beginning to outrun the attackers. Arrows still came whirring at them, rattling to rest outside and in; an occasional lance *thwunked* harmlessly against the side of the car; and now and then a fire arrow would come their way—but the intensity of the attack was lessening. Most of the windows on both sides were broken and the rest of the passengers continued to cower in the aisle. Two men had been injured, though neither seriously. Still, all of it could have been taking place in another car, another train, for all the attention the players accorded it.

It was Horne's deal. He raked in the cards, skillfully palming the two aces from the winning hand, raising his palm to his face and letting them slide down into his cuff to join the third ace already lodged there. Two hands later he was dealt a pair of kings. He palmed away his other three cards, substituted his aces, and bumped the pot up to nearly eight thousand dollars. The judge and the drummer stayed and contributed handsomely up to his last raise before dropping out. Alice saw his thousand-dollar raise and raised him an equal amount.

He paused to consider the situation. His mind's eye went back over the previous three hands. In all three something was missing: one card, a small one.

The four!

Not a single four of any suit had shown, not in the winning or losing hands, not in the discards. His heart sank. His confidence in his aces full of kings had encouraged him to boldness, and depleted his supply of chips to under twelve hundred dollars' worth. He pondered. He could give her the hand and save a thousand, or he could call and keep her honest. Calling would be foolhardy, he reasoned, a violation of his every professional instinct. An arrow flew between the four of them at eye level and *thwunked*, shuddering to rest in the window post opposite.

"Mr. Richardson?" asked Alice politely.

Horne cleared his throat and tossed in his hand. Reduced to two hundred dollars he'd be unable to stay and play even the most powerful hand.

"Out."

She lay her hand facedown and pulled in her winnings.

"You could beat my five-to-nine straight," said the judge, "you could, couldn't you?"

She flicked the ash from her cigar and smiled demurely. "With all due respect, your Honor, you didn't pay to see."

"I didn't, still this is a friendly game. None of us is professional."

"That's true."

The judge had laid his bony fingers on her hand, laying backs up. Again she smiled, then nodded. He turned over her cards. Nausea struck and gripped Horne's innards. His upper body suddenly felt as if it were melting. She had taken his pot with a full house: fours over queens!

"Oh, my God . . ."

"Mr. Richardson?" she asked.

"Nothing."

For the first time since the attack he glanced out the window. The Indians had stopped their shrilling and shooting, and the handful that had pursued the train to this point were dropping away one by one. The passengers ducking in the aisle rose and returned to their seats, and Horne recounted his chips for the sixth time in the last two minutes, feeling her dark eyes staring at him. And she was smiling at him. In sympathy or triumph? he wondered drearily.

"What did you have, Mr. Richardson?" asked the judge.

"Nothing much."

"You stayed; you raised three times."

"Your deal, Judge."

Win a few, lose a few, thought Horne, though in this instance he hadn't "lost" to her, he'd given her the pot, intimidated by her reputation. Very bad form on his part. Uncle Perry would dress him down in lavender if he ever found out. The first weapon in the professional gambler's arsenal was skill, the second, spleen, gumption, bluff born of supreme self-confidence. You were supposed to awe your opposition, whoever it might be, not be awed by him/her.

Poker Alice Ivers, T. G. Horne—two of a kind, save in one respect. She had fallen into gambling after her husband died. She needed money, but wasn't destitute. He, on the other hand, had never known anything but destitution before taking up the trade. From the day he was born to the day he left home, the rat of poverty gnawed unceasingly at his soul. He had never been given a bought Christmas present. There was never any money to buy anything apart from food and used clothing. He had never owned a pair of shoes that hadn't been worn previously. It was his Uncle Perry who had rescued him, put him on his feet, taught him his skills, spoon-fed him confidence, courage, and daring without which no professional gambler can make his way.

He had been born and brought up in the gray and god-forsaken country of Oklahoma. His father had been a farmer, struggling from the first day Horne could remember to the day of his death to wrest a crop from the dust that substituted for soil. He vividly remembered one day that typified his entire boyhood on the farm. Dawn broke; in the mussel-gray sky a faint red disk appeared, and as the day moved forward, it grew feebler, giving way to gloom. In the hot, stinging air the wind lamented the passing of the dried and wretched corn. At midday the wind rested. The dust it had raised filled the air like fog, hanging immobile, and the sun revived, reappearing as red as the heart of a fire. He saw his father standing in the doorway of the ramshackle house watching the slow death of his hopes. The corn was ruined, as it had been the year before and the year before that. It was a sight he had become used to, a result to be expected. What was unexpected, discouraging, even frightening, was his father's face. In his eyes, the slackness of his jaw, his inability to speak, was complete and utter defeat. His heart was empty of optimism, the last shred of hope had vanished, he had given up. For three years he had worked to evening exhaustion preparing the soil, planting, nurturing the new shoots, weeding, devoting the care one might accord prize roses to each struggling stalk, only to see his crop rise and fall, conquered by too much rain or too little, or sun, dust, hail, wind, a conspiracy of the elements. They took turns bullying the crop, destroying it.

Failure finally broke his father; it didn't matter that their neighbors suffered similarly, that there were valid excuses for the crop's death, that it was not within his or anyone's power to prevent it. There it was, the rubble of his dream.

Out of failure came poverty, so grinding, so relentlessly oppressive—with its half-meals and skipped meals, hungry nights, ragged clothing, the cup of despair and its bitter taste, his father's eyes and finally his death—that he'd vowed, standing over his father's grave, that he would never let the same fate capture and conquer him. He would find other dragons to battle.

The one he found, thanks to Perry, Perry's own, defied conquering; the battle was continuous and there were times when it exhausted him, times when he suffered frightful punishment, when his arm wearied, his sword slipped from his grasp, but all things considered, he enjoyed it. He relished the challenge; the setbacks, as in this instance, were only temporary. Back he'd come, back to the attack, forcing the dragon to give way. There'd be another pot tomorrow, a bigger one, he'd win it. The dragon would capitulate, withdraw, nurse its wounds, and return for another go.

He would not die flush, or broke, but somewhere between. The important thing, the one knowledge that sustained him, was that he could look in his mirror till the day he died and never see anything like the expression on his father's face that day he stood in the doorway and looked out over his ravaged crop.

The Hotel Meadowlark was not particularly majestic in appearance—oversized and rambling would better describe it; it was by far the largest building on the street; it was also fairly new, and the overstuffed chairs in the lobby still retained the odor of well-oiled leather. The four potted palms were healthy, cigar smoke did not hang from the ceiling in an odoriferous cloud, cleanliness and order reigned throughout. The clerk was busy pigeonholing mail when the bishop walked in. Two loungers occupied chairs: one a gentleman who looked well into his eighties and whose palsy set his copy of the *Rocky Mountain News* rattling in his hands; the other a handsome man a third his age attired in a black broadcloth suit with a plain magenta silk vest. His sole accessory of distinction was a Jürgensen watch with a diamond in its stem and attached to a gold chain. The man with the newspaper lowered it to size up Bishop Winfield passing him; the other lounger, turning his attention to igniting a cheroot, took no notice of him. The bishop nodded to the desk clerk and ascended the stairs to the second floor, moving down the hallway to the corner room, overlooking the street. He entered, leaving the door open. Moments later the man with the Jurgensen watch appeared.

"Perry!"

"Ssssssh." Bishop Winfield closed his door. "Bishop Bolton Winfield, if you don't mind." He smiled and clapped an affectionate hand on the other's shoulder. "Welcome to Fodder City, T.G., and before we start, let's drop both Horne and Richardson. You'll need another name entirely."

"Edward Tillinghast has a nice ring."

"A bit flowery."

"What do you call Pericles Jubal Youngquist? Edward Z. Tillinghast. Sounds like authority, just right for a bank examiner."

"Sit, make yourself comfortable, we've a lot of catching up. I'd offer you a drink, but Bishop Bolton Winfield doesn't keep liquor on hand."

"Why bishop? Wouldn't an ordinary clergyman suit?"

Pericles Jubal Youngquist—uncle and mentor to his visitor, T. G. Horne—had moved to the window to look down into the street.

"I need clerical rank on this job. The local clergy has to look up to me. Before I tell you the setup, there are two things we've got to agree on: first, you must find yourself another hotel; and we don't know each other, not yet, not until I bump into you at the bank. I'll make certain I'm with one of my colleagues-of-the-cloth at the time. And it might be nice if you were introduced to us by the president of the bank."

"Whatever you say."

"We're in the works, T.G. A lot has been accomplished in just two days. We've gotten our license to operate, the tickets have been printed and have gone on sale. They're a dollar apiece, six for five dollars, twenty for sixteen. Promotion is under way."

"What's the grand prize?"

"I'm keeping it flexible. We're starting with fifty thousand. As the money rolls in, we'll raise it accordingly and post the raise in front of the bank every morning. Excellent gimmick for fanning the fires of interest. There'll be five ten-thousand-dollar prizes, five five-thousand, and fifty one-hundreds. We've already opened a special account at the bank. You'll be appointed to keep an eye on it."

"As a visiting bank examiner."

"Exactly."

"Why me, an outsider?"

"Why not you? Who's better qualified? Bank examiner is a position of trust, my boy. It'll be up to you to reek of reliance, honesty, integrity. Keep clear of the gaming tables while you're here. Bank examiners don't gamble in public, so put your poker skills to bed and keep them there."

"Don't talk to me about poker."

He recounted his humiliating introduction to Poker Alice Ivers en route.

Perry had no sympathy for him. "What on earth made you think you could get the best of a four-star pro like her, male ego?"

"Oh, shut up! I was holding my own. I got a little reckless, then a little gutless. She didn't break me, if that's what's worrying you."

"Not at all. If she did, I could always manage a loan. Say twenty percent?"

"You're all heart. This special bank account, why doesn't the president watch it himself? Wouldn't it be a public service and lend a touch of dignity, community pride, something?"

"President Flynn doesn't want to be bothered, doesn't want the responsibility."

He told Horne about the meeting with the five clergymen. Horne listened without comment, but with a serious expression masking his handsome face. Now and then he would pluck at one end of his mustache, a sign to Perry that something was troubling him.

"What is it?" he asked.

"My conscience, I guess."

"Shame on you! You call yourself a professional?"

"Perry, you know me. I'm game for any scam; nothing's too big or too outrageous, but taking the church to the cleaners . . ."

"Great Caesar's ghost, is that what you think? That I'd be party to such unscrupulous deviltry? You think I have no conscience? Perish forbid; I'd never be able to live with myself. No question we're duping them, but we're not cheating. All we're interested in is the winning tickets; what's left after expenses, after the prize money's paid out, will be equally divided among the five denominations, and rest assured, there'll be a bundle, likely twice our take. T.G., you surprise me, the mere thought that I would deliberately bilk any religion is most insulting, distressing."

"Sorry."

"I may be a con artist but I'm no thief."

The distinction between the two was a trifle blurry in Horne's mind, but he let it pass without further comment.

"There's one other thing, Perry. You say a lot of the big names are in town fleecing the miners. Colonel Charlie Norton knows me by sight."

"So? Get hold of him and tell him what's going on.

No need to be specific, just say you've got something going. He won't sandbag you as long as we don't stick our hands in his pockets. Besides, as I remember, he owes you one. From that five-card stud game in Sonora two years ago; the Ostrowski brothers would have caught him with aces up his sleeve if you hadn't 'accidentally' tipped over that bottle of rotgut and temporarily broken up the game. Out of the kindness of your heart you gave him a chance to clean out his sleeves. At the time he practically overflowed with gratitude.

"As for the other biggies, none of them knows us by sight, we don't know them. T.G., please don't start erecting obstacles. There are no real problems, nothing we can't deal with. The beauty of it is everything's on the up and up right up to the night of the drawing. With a little sleight-of-hand we can walk away from this thing with eighty or ninety thousand. If it takes off, maybe double that."

"Who are you getting to do the drawing?"

"I've been in touch with an old, very dear, and trusted friend, Prunella Watley."

"Oh, my God, can't you do better than that!"

Perry's nostrils flared with indignation; he drew in a breath sharply. "Prunella happens to be one of the most skilled sleight-of-hand artists in the West."

"Prunella also happens to be one of the biggest lushes. Aren't you afraid she'll turn up dead drunk? Even not turn up at all because she's out cold?"

"I most certainly am not! We all of us have our pecadilloes, my boy. There's no cause for worry, I'll keep an eye on her."

"Just keep her out of the bottle. All we need is to work our heads off all the way up to the drawing night and stand helplessly by and watch Prunie turn it into disaster."

"I said I'll be responsible."

"Somebody'd better be."

"All right! It's settled. Come over here."

Horne joined his uncle at the window, flinging his cheroot butt out and arcing into the horse trough below.

"See that sign down the corner? MacIvitty's Lodgings. You'll be comfortable there. Get on over and get yourself settled. From now on until we're introduced we steer clear of each other. If you want to meet for any reason, hang a rubber band around my doorknob. There's an abandoned sawmill about four miles east of town. We can meet there at, say, eleven at night. I don't know why it should be necessary, but if something should pop up . . ."

"You're sore."

"I'm not."

"Perry, we can't be too careful. Isn't that what you're always telling me? We're on our own here. We don't know a soul except Colonel Charlie. Frankly, Prunella really does worry me."

"Didn't I say it's all settled, I'd be responsible?" Perry relaxed; his stern expression dissolved into an affable smile. "It'll go off smooth as silk, see if it doesn't."

Horne nodded, at the same time groaning inwardly, yielding to superstition. In his experience such cocksuredness invariably jinxed the best-laid plans of men.

2

Posing as a bank examiner would be a new role for Horne. He did not see that it called for any special expertise or equipment, apart from a fountain pen and a pair of prop spectacles to give him the look of a mathematical wizard. He was preparing to leave his room at MacIvitty's Lodgings to walk to the bank and introduce himself to President Flynn when a knock sounded at his door. He opened. There stood a burly, middle-aged man in a dapper white linen suit and hat and string tie with hands emerging from his cuffs the size of small chickens.

"T.G.!" he boomed.

"Sssssh, for God's sakes, come in, come in."

"Sorry, boy."

"Charlie Norton, you old reprobate."

"Cunnel Nawton, if y'all don't mind." He seized and completely covered Horne's hand and practically shook it from his wrist. "Ah spotted y'all walking in this dump. Whatcha' doing heah, anyhow?" He winked broadly. "Come to town to pluck a few chickens?"

"Not exactly."

He boomed laughter. "Then what 'zactly? What else y'all good at, ah mean outta bed? Ha ha. Wheah's old pinchface P. J.?"

"He's here."

The colonel gaped, stiffened, and impaled him with one finger. "Ah know, you two are dealing the lottery, i'n that so? Y'all got to be. Bless youh lahcenous hahts, y'all sure 'nough come to the right place. Theah's moh silvah money floating 'round this town than halfa Colorado. Ah been cleaning up at three-card monte."

"Isn't that a little dangerous?"

"Not playin' 'em one atta time it ain't. It's the group activities that are dangerous. Not half an houh ago Riley Grannan got himself all shot up over at the Artesia Saloon. Miner claimed he was bottom-dealing himself. Old Riley's in a bad way, bleedin' like blazes, they don't know if he'll live. These double-jackers can get mighty mean when they catch somebody snaking the game. Hey, T.G., how's about cuttin' this old boy in on youh action, whatta you say?"

"Not a chance, Charlie. Perry and I can handle it nicely, thank you."

Charlie's face fell slowly into the hurt expression of a five-year-old, complete with lower lip pushing against upper. "Theah must be something ah can help with."

"Nothing, thank you. What's the matter with your three-card monte?"

"Ah need a change, boy."

"I'm sorry."

Charlie's eyes narrowed. "Ah know how to keep mah mouth shut."

"Are you threatening me, Charlie? Don't. Just keep our little secret among the three of us, okay? Fair warning."

"Oh, hell, okay. Ah was just funning y'all, testing."

"Thanks for dropping in; I don't think it'd be good for us to be seen together, so let's make this hello and good-bye, okay? Maybe we can get together down in Sonora later in the year."

"Sonora, yeah. Ah remember y'all tipped that bottle ovah. That was a neah one, ah musta' sweated off ten pounds that aftahnoon."

"I'll be seeing you, Charlie, and good luck with your monte game."

Rev. Cletus O. Miller and Father Patrick Dunphy

hurried up the street to catch up with Bishop Winfield. Both were excited.

"Tickets are going like hotcakes," burst Rev. Miller.

"One of my flock bought fifty," exclaimed Father Dunphy.

"We've just come from Pastor Lacklund's. His wife has agreed to devote all her free time to your brainchild."

"Doing what, pray tell?"

"Overseeing the special account at the bank."

"What?"

"She works at the bank, you know. She's right there all day long."

Father Dunphy beamed and nodded. "She's readying a special account book and everything. She says she'll be able to give us each day's total sales and the overall total every afternoon at five-fifteen after the bank closes."

Bishop Winfield could feel his cheeks tingling. Here was an obstacle erected that T.G. had nothing to do with! He glanced up the way. There he was, spectacles and all, crossing the street, heading for the bank to introduce himself as the recently arrived bank examiner.

"They say she's an absolute wizard with figures," said Rev. Miller. "Have you met her yet?"

"I haven't had the pleasure."

"You will," said Father Dunphy. "Walk with us to my place, I want to get my pipe, then we'll march you over to the bank and introduce you."

He certainly should meet the lady, thought Perry; he'd have to know her to take care of her. On second thought, it didn't seem right to poison, garrote, or otherwise permanently dispatch a minister's wife. It was as bad as killing a minister! Maybe it wouldn't have to be that drastic; all he really had to do was take her out of circulation for a while. . . .

Horne shook hands with D. Lennox Flynn, president of the Fodder City Miners and Merchants Bank. Ushered into Flynn's office by a Mrs. Lacklund, Horne found him relaxed and smiling, but when the lady introduced him as Mr. Edward Tillinghast, "the examiner," a sudden and surprising change came over Flynn's shining pink features, and even his bald head appeared to redden. His relaxed, even jaunty air gave way to nervousness. He began to lick his lips, his eyes darted about in their sockets, and he started picking at the hairs on the back of his left hand.

"You want to see our books?"

"The Territorial Banking Commission does," replied Horne airily.

"Very well. Mrs. Lacklund, please see that Mr. Tillinghast is given everything he needs. The bank will be pleased to extend you every courtesy, sir; I'm sure Mrs. Lacklund can answer any questions you may have. I'll be here if you need me."

Horne got the distinct impression that he wanted him out of his office as fast as he could move. He followed Mrs. Lacklund out and down behind the row of tellers' cages to a corner table near the vault door.

"All the records are in the vault except current," she said. She got the books out for him. She was short and threatening to become portly, but her smile was pleasant, she was friendly, and her voice had a lovely, musical timbre. Were he asked to describe her in a few words, "young matron" would have come to mind, he thought.

"I'll work my way up to current. I'll want to start a year back, if you don't mind."

"That far?" She lowered her voice. "Is something . . ."

"Wrong? Do you think there might be?"

"Oh, no, no, no . . ." She looked puzzled. "But the last examiner was here less than six months ago."

"I know, but we can't be too thorough, can we?" He gave her a martyred look. "We do have to answer for our mistakes, you know. No harm in going over the numbers a second time. You can be sure the next chap will go over what I'll be covering."

He assumed his role for her benefit, sitting, diligently polishing his spectacles, getting out his Columbian No. 2 solid-gold 16-carat fountain pen. He polished the point briefly with a bit of cambric and held it to the light to examine it, polished it again to remove an imaginary speck, and pumped it full in the inkwell. He could feel her eyes on him and continued to strive to convey an impression of quietly fierce dedication to exactitude. Not so much as a decimal point would escape his searching eye.

He went to work, jotting down figures and cranking away at the Sholes adding machine she had provided him. Customers came and went; the hot, dry, dusty day worked its sluggard's way toward midafternoon. Three men came in; all wore clerical garb. Mrs. Lacklund had just brought Horne a glass of water. He had turned on his stool to accept it and thank her; he recognized one of the three clerics and watched as another called Mrs. Lacklund over and introduced her. The four of them began chatting amiably. Horne strained his ears, but could hear nothing. He turned back to his work. There'd be no introduction today. Attempting one would be awkward, ill-suited to the occasion.

When the bank closed and he left for the day, he went back to his room to find a rubber band around his doorknob.

On Sunday afternoon, the fourth day into the lottery, but one on which no tickets were sold, no cards publicly turned in town and no dice thrown, Bishop Winfield had been invited to afternoon tea by Mrs. Lacklund. He considered arming himself for his visit with pills or a powder of some sort capable of inducing a violent though not lethal disorder of the stomach. He reasoned that if the lady were confined to her bed for a time, someone else would be pressed into service to attend to the special account and keep it up to date.

Ticket sales on Saturday had more than doubled those of the two previous days. A tidal wave of response appeared to be sweeping the area. Requests for tickets accompanied by money were arriving from nearby Sundance, from as far away as Alva and Aladdin up north, and even from across the South Dakota border, from Bellefource, Sturgis, and Deadwood. At the rate the news was spreading, by Wednesday of the following week the entire northeast corner of the territory would be clamoring for tickets. By Sunday morning the grand prize had risen to $70,000 on the ten-foot-high announcement board erected outside the bank.

It was absolutely vital that Horne be in charge of the special account so that he would be the one to dispense the money to the winning ticket holders the morning after the drawing. If he was not, the bottom would drop out of the whole scam. When he entered the bank in the morning, he would have in his possession his and Perry's tickets and their stubs palmed and "selected" by Prunella Watley the night before. Fictitious names would of course be used on the held-out stubs to protect against any possible confusion. Immediately upon entering the bank, before the doors were opened to the waiting linc of winners, Horne would count out and pocket the total amount won by his holdouts.

He would dispense the legitimate winners' prize money, he would total the results and cnter them in the book, he would close the book. It would then be turned over to the county sheriff for safekeeping. If anyone suspected chicanery and wished to examine the books, they need only ask the sheriff for permission. They would find nothing whatsoever to confirm their suspicions.

Rev. Miller joined Bishop Winfield and Pastor and Mrs. Lacklund for tea. The Baptist church parsonage was small, the parlor—the largest room in the house—barely long enough to accommodate a standard-sized dice table, mused the bishop as he was ushered in. Mrs. Lacklund offered a choice of teas: orange pekoe, gunpowder, or her particular favorite, chamomile. Bishop Winfield requested the last-named. As he watched the lady sip from her cup, misgivings assailed him. Why hadn't he found the courage to fetch along something that would lay her low for a few days? He sniffed audibly; he knew the answer to that: it wasn't his style; whatever the cause, whatever the urgency, he could never do such a thing. Dear me, he thought, what if he were to accidentally kill the poor thing?

He watched the looks and listened to the snatches of conversation that passed between husband and wife. They seemed to be happily married; there seemed no chance she would leave him. And dowdy as she was, she couldn't possibly have a secret lover who might run away with her.

Fortunately, he still had time to come up with something, time until the night of the drawing next Friday. Nearly a week. Perhaps she might come down with an illness, requiring her to take to her bed. Slim chance of that; she looked discouragingly healthy. Maybe she'd have an accident; a simple broken leg would restrict her to quarters.

He sipped and sighed inwardly.

"Where are you from originally, Bishop?" she asked.

"Wayzata, Minnesota. By the waters of the Minnetonka."

"Hiawatha. How romantic. I so adore woods and lakes. When I was a child, I loved to go camping. But Hildreth is a city boy."

"Oh, what city, may I ask?"

"Alton, Illinois," said Hildreth.

Mrs. Lacklund laughed lightly. "He finds the great outdoors . . ."

"Annoying, my dear, the bugs, mosquitoes, poison ivy, branches snapping in one's face."

"My poor Hildreth. My husband's health is not good, Bishop. He has an ulcer, you know; we have to be very careful what we put in our tummy, don't we, dear?"

Bishop Winfield perked up at the word "ulcer," held his breath, and listened intently. But there was no further elaboration. He needed none. So the good pastor had an ulcer, did he? Being a Baptist, he didn't drink regardless. But he had to eat.

And if he got sick, he'd have to go to bed.

And if he went to bed, he'd need someone to care for him.

Horne would have to make more than a week's work out of his examination. He saw this as no problem; he worked slowly, meticulously, going over and over a figure once arrived at, and he was forever stopping to clean his pen point or polish his spectacles. Bishop Winfield came into the bank Monday afternoon with Rev. Miller, who brought him back to Flynn's office to introduce him. Horne followed them, pausing in the doorway, letting Rev. Miller finish his introductions and excusing himself for interrupting.

"I'm so sorry, gentlemen. Mr. Flynn, I can't seem to find the foreclosure figures on the Hemingway property. March sixth and seventh . . ."

"Mrs. Lacklund knows."

"Of course, forgive me for interrupting."

"No harm done," said Rev. Miller, "Mr. "

"This is Mr. Edward Tillinghast, the bank examiner," said Flynn. "Mr. Tillinghast, Reverend Cletus Miller, Bishop Bolton Winfield."

"Delighted to meet you," said the bishop.

"Did I see you in church yesterday?" asked Rev. Miller.

"I'm Presbyterian," said Tillinghast.

"Ahhh, Reverend Hollings. Prince of a fellow. Gives an excellent sermon, doesn't he?"

"Spellbinding."

All four chatted for a few minutes more before Mr. Tillinghast excused himself and returned to work. Walking away, he heard Rev. Miller.

"Pleasant fellow. Must be a mathematical genius to be a bank examiner, eh?"

"He seems to know his business," responded Flynn.

After work Horne drifted about town, noting the placards and the two slender banners stretching over the main street announcing the lottery. It seemed to be the topic of conversation.

"I got me twenty tickets, and I mean to buy at least twenty more."

"Grand prize is up to seventy-five thousand."

"If I win, I'll never swing another pick long as I live, s'help me."

"It could get up to quarter of a million by Friday."

"Not that high. Higher, but not no quarter of a million."

He went into the Artesia Saloon for a drink. Col. Norton's comment about Riley Grannan came back to him as he espied a poker game in progress. He wondered how Riley was faring, wondered if he were still alive. Had lottery fever not seized the town, his shooting would have been on everybody's tongue. As it was, nobody seemed to know or care if he were alive or dead.

Lottery tickets were available at the bar. It ran a good forty feet and kept two bartenders busy. No fewer than six spittoons were strategically placed inside the brass rail. The ceiling was fashioned of squares of pressed tin; four white, glass-domed lamps hung from it. The far wall displayed a nude intended by the artist to appear voluptuous, but looking just plain overweight, with a face as round as a plate to match her girth. The roulette wheel stood idle.

A faro game was under way, four players and the dealer working at top speed, averaging two wagers a minute. Bettors could back a card of any rank simply by setting their chips on a reproduction of the card fixed to the tabletop. Bets on two cards at once were placed between the cards. Suits were irrelevant. After the bets were placed, the dealer dealt the cards from the box. The players backing the first card dealt lost; bets placed on the second card won. Bets on other cards were either left for the next play or taken back by the players. If a pair was dealt, the bank took half the money stacked on the paired card.

Horne watched briefly, looking for cheating. The game seemed to be on the up and up; the box wasn't rigged, the dealer slid only one card out at a time. The deck did not look crooked. There was no tinhorn short-changing on bets or attempts to confuse the players as to the cards that had already been played.

Still, he could come back an hour later to a different dealer and see rampant cheating unnoticed by the players. The Will and Finck Company marketed nineteen different kinds of dealing boxes, of which three were honest. Boxes rigged with springs, levers, and sliding plates with names like sand-tell, coffee-mill, end squeeze, needle squeeze, and horse box permitted the dealer to deal or withhold whatever cards he pleased sold for as much as two hundred dollars. No game was more popular in the West, not even poker.

He kibitzed one of the two poker games. He detected no cheating, but a skillful dealer took great pains not to display his wares. Sight of the idle roulette wheel, the faro game, the poker games, stirred his competitive juices. Every time he walked into a gambling casino, even a saloon offering nothing more than a bird cage, an open-topped dice tub or dice chute sitting on the bar, he felt the same stirrings in his gut and his heart beat faster. Gambling was his favorite drink, life's chief delight, his first love. Had an objective observer told him it was a chronic illness, Horne would have laughed in his face. He would have also privately agreed. He gambled so much and was so good at it, so successful, he couldn't quit if his life depended on it. The danger was one spur: the satisfaction of winning, the inherent challenge the other.

First, last, and always, his game was poker. He disdained advantage tools as cumbersome, unreliable, and unnecessary. He had never even tried a sleeve holdout, breastplate holdout, pointed "bug," a waist bag with a spring-loaded frame manipulated by one's leg, the knee-operated Kepplinger holdout, a holdout vest. They were for some, but not him. He relied on skillful hands, practicing two hours a day every day to keep his moves at the peak of sharpness. Palming, stacking, crimping, bottom-dealing, all required constant practice. He never resorted to marked cards, trimmed cards, strippers, coolers, or any other type of doctored deck.

He had one drink at the bar and left. He couldn't stay another thirty seconds, so powerful was the urge to take the empty chair in the poker game in the corner under the glazed eyes of the amply endowed nude in the giltwood frame. He could have cleaned out all five players in an hour, and honestly, they were that poor, that reckless. And all appeared well-heeled.

But Perry was right: bank examiners don't gamble.

He passed the colonel in the street. They looked through each other. Horne thought as he walked by that the man was a pro, he wouldn't muddy another pro's well.

3

By Wednesday evening the grand prize reached $100,000, twice the initial amount allotted, twice the amount of James Monroe Pattee's fabled and cleverly rigged Wyoming lottery held some years earlier. The Lottery King, as Pattee called himself, raked in approximately seven million dollars in all of his ventures in the territory. Perry's hopes for success rested on Pattee's experience. Tickets in the Wyoming lottery's monthly drawing numbered more than half a million. Each month more than seventy thousand prizes were offered, totaling $200,000 to $275,000. The ratio of prizes to tickets was reasonable; unfortunately, only thirty-five prizes were worth more than a hundred dollars. Investing one dollar in a ticket, seventy thousand of the winners had a chance to collect fifty cents. These "lucky" individuals were notified by Pattee that it would cost more to send them their winnings than the value of their prize. He then generously offered to send instead a sharc of stock worth ten dollars in his Bullion Gold and Silver Mining Company; he would engage them to act as his agents, for which they would receive a free share for every five they sold at two dollars per share.

His biggest edge over the Grand Lottery of Crook County was his large-scale advertising campaign. He ran frequent advertisements in such distant newspapers as the *New York Herald Tribune*. When reformers from out of the territory got after him, he slipped out of Wyoming and set up a new operation in Canada.

Wyoming's unhappy experience with the Lottery King

in no way dampened people's enthusiasm for lotteries in general. One could get rich a good deal quicker winning the grand prize than digging for silver, punching cattle, or herding sheep. And get rich quick was every man's dream.

Prunella Watley arrived in Fodder City Wednesday evening. Perry met her stage. She was discernably longer in the tooth than she had been the last time their paths had crossed. She called herself forty-nine, but had for upward of ten years, so her true age was not hard to ascertain. Within the frame of her black yarn fascinator was a square, onetime pretty face with dyed brunette curls fringing her forehead. Crow's-feet had arrived and twin age lines angled down each side of her mouth. She resisted the onset of age, or rather tried to mask it with a liberal application of makeup. Underneath was a heavy drinker's florid complexion, and her voice was well below alto.

Rev. Miller and Rev. Grier accompanied Bishop Winfield to the stage depot to meet his sister. Prunella may have displayed the ravages of the rough life she led and the years she had accumulated, but she was a perfect lady—that is, she essayed the role with considerable conviction. Traces of her eastern finishing-school education gave her an accent that was very close to British; her posture and walk were elegant, and she exuded dignity from every pore.

She had come all the way from Sacramento, a grueling ride.

"Another orphanage, my dear?" asked the bishop.

"Number eighteen, Bolton."

"How do you do it?"

"Dear me, it's not that difficult. One arrives in town with the proper references and introductions to friends of friends, and almost before you know it, the word is around town of the purpose of one's visit and the contributions begin rolling in. Mayor Clendennon pledged five thousand dollars. Other wealthy Sacramentoans refused to be outdone. When it's finished, the Sacramento

County Home for Foundlings will be four buildings in one with accommodations for more than seven hundred little people."

"What a praiseworthy endeavor, dear lady," gushed Rev. Grier.

"One does what one can in this needy world, Reverend."

"Amos, please . . ."

She smiled, clutched her fascinator under the chin, and lowered her eyes demurely. The bishop talked excitedly about the lottery. The three clergymen escorted Prunella to the Hotel Meadowlark, where she pleaded fatigue and, parting company with them, went directly to bed. The three sat in the lobby for a few minutes talking before the bishop retired to his room.

"She's spent her entire adult life traveling about the country doing good works," the bishop said proudly. "I only wish she wouldn't overdo it so."

"Is she not well?" asked Rev. Grier.

"Not ill, but not robust. And she works like a stevedore. I'm so glad she accepted my invitation. She needs the rest. I hope she'll decide to stay longer than the week she's planned."

"An amazing woman," said Rev. Grier. "Eighteen orphanages."

"In less than four years. And hard as she works, she refuses to take a penny for expenses. Fortunately, the interest from a rather sizable trust fund set up by Grandfather Winfield provides for her needs. I can't wait to look through her scrapbook. It's been over a year since I last saw it."

He went on to explain what he called her "sole concession to pride," her scrapbook filled with snapshots and newspaper clippings describing her philanthropic triumphs.

"I've a dandy idea," exclaimed Rev. Grier. "She'd be perfect for the job of selecting the tickets on the night of the drawing. Do you think she would?"

"I can ask her," said the bishop. "She's really quite

shy, but if it's a good cause—and what could be better than this—I know she'd be happy to pitch in."

"Please ask her," said Rev. Miller.

"I shall, I shall." He fisted a yawn, excused himself and went up to bed.

As Bishop Winfield reached the second floor, the spring returned to his step. He knocked on the door of the room next to his own. Prunella appeared in a Japanese kimono, her hair bound up, her makeup removed, her face heavily caked with night cream.

"Pericles, you old scalawag!" She threw her arms around him, crushing him to her, squeezing the air from his lungs, leaving him gasping. "How was I?"

"Splendid, dear girl, top form. By the way, you've just been unanimously chosen to draw the winning tickets."

"How flattering." She plunked down on the bed. "Sit, tell me all."

He did so, finishing with the question on the subject uppermost in her mind.

"How much do you want, my dear?"

"Five hundred plus expenses, of course. The stage from Cheyenne was eighty-eight dollars and I'm heading back there when we're finished."

"Five hundred is exactly five times as much as I had in mind."

"Perry, Perry, Perry . . ."

"Yes? Yes? Yes?"

"What are you paying for? The golden key to the whole operation. I'll be palming your grand-prize winning stub and a few others. When these two gifted hands go to work, not a single eyebrow rises in suspicion. You know that, you know I'm the best. Why else drag me all the way up here?"

"True."

"I'll take the hundred."

He started in astonishment. He had never known her to settle on price first shot out of the barrel. She was expert at wearing down the purchaser, wearying him so he finally gave in to her terms.

"I . . ." he began, flustered.

"For old times' sake I'll forgo dickering." She dug into her opened suitcase and brought out a bottle. "Let's drink to success."

He frowned. "Prunella, this deal has a small stipulation. No drinking until we're all wrapped up."

"What's the matter, Perry? Afraid I'll turn up drunk at the drawing?"

"Of course not! How could you even think such a thing?"

"I won't, I'm a pro. I drink a little, but never on the job."

Her tone suggested indignation. He studied her slitted eyes.

"By all means, let's do have a drink," he said, rubbing his hands together briskly. "A toast to success."

Friday arrived. Lottery fever gripped every man, woman, and child in and for miles around Fodder City. Bishop Winfield advised that the grand prize be kept at the hundred-thousand figure. The other members of the lottery committee, the five clergymen, agreed. As the clock moved inexorably forward toward the hour of nine and the drawing, the bishop's heart beat faster. And at the same time worry took root in his stomach and began to spread.

In the middle of the afternoon he called on Prunella and told her of his concern.

"T.G. *has* to be in charge of the special account. Has to be in the bank bright and early tomorrow morning, prepared to pay off the winners."

"And ring in your winning stubs and collect your money. That'll be his first order of business."

"That's right. The thing is, Reverend Hildreth Lacklund's wife, Henrietta, is presently in charge of the special account. Unless we can get rid of her sometime between now and tomorrow morning, T. G.'ll be left out in the cold and we'll be in serious trouble."

"He can't just take over the payoff," Prunella said. "That'd be very awkward."

"It'd be impossible."

"What are you going to do?"

"There's to be a dinner meeting of the committee at six tonight. I'm going to have to take the bull by the horns and lay the lady's husband low. It shouldn't be hard. I'll slip something into his soup or whatever, make him ill; he'll go home to bed and his doting wife will have to take over care of him. She will, I'm sure, in which case she won't show up at the bank in the morning."

"That sounds fine."

"On second thought, it could be risky. Lacklund has an ulcer. If I slip him Jimson weed, it'll probably kill him—as will toadstool, wood alcohol, any number of substances. I can hardly murder the poor man just to get his wife out of the game. If I could only make him sick overnight and into tomorrow, sick enough to put him to bed and keep him there without endangering his life."

"That's easy; a simple solution of soap and water should do it."

The sun came up on his face; his eyes widened, brightened, and twinkled. "Great Caesar's ghost, you're a genius. The perfect solution."

"In his coffee, his soup . . ."

"I wouldn't need much. I could carry it in a pill bottle."

"He'll feel deathly ill; he'll probably throw up. In any case he'll head for home and bed."

"He will, he will! Prunella, darling, you've saved the day."

She laughed. "No extra charge."

"You're worth your weight in gold."

"Sssh. You keep that up and we'll have to make an adjustment in my contract."

Promptly at six o'clock Bishop Winfield, Reverends

Miller, Grier, Hollings, and Father Dunphy assembled at the Fodder City Restaurant for their dinner meeting.

"Has anyone seen Reverend Lacklund?" asked the bishop.

Father Dunphy whacked the bowl of his pipe against the ashtray. "He can't make it."

The bishop started. "But . . . but he has to. I mean, why can't he?"

The tables near theirs were empty. The dining room was only half-filled. A waiter stood in his white jacket and bow tie, holding menus, staring fixedly at the bishop, mutely asking to be summoned. Winfield shook his head.

"Oh, nothing's wrong," said Dunphy, "not with Hildreth, that is."

"It's Henrietta," said Rev. Miller. "She's leaving town. Going down to Denver to visit her sister. Hildreth is driving her to Moorcroft to catch the train. It all came up rather suddenly."

From shock Bishop Winfield lurched into amazement, quickly supplanted by relief.

"You don't say."

"She'll probably be away all next week."

"But who'll take over for her at the bank? First thing tomorrow morning the winners have to be paid. They'll be lined up at the door before the bank opens."

"We could ring in Lennox Flynn," Father Dunphy suggested.

Rev. Hollings shook his head. "He's already made it clear that he wants nothing to do with the lottery. It's not a problem, is it? Can't one of the tellers pay off the winners? The money's right there."

"It's got to be someone with a little more financial acumen," said Rev. Miller. "By golly, I've got it! That fellow—what's his name?—the bank examiner."

"Mr. Tillinghast," said the bishop.

"He'd be perfect for the job. He strikes me as the soul of conscientiousness. The very sort we need."

"Excellent idea," the bishop said. "If you gentlemen agree, I'd be glad to approach him."

Rev. Grier, Rev. Hollings, and Father Dunphy had no objections. All five dined on roast pheasant. Bishop Winfield ate heartily, savoring every morsel. Now and then his right hand wandered to the pocket of his jacket. In it was a small bottle of soapy water tightly corked. There it would remain until he disposed of it.

All the way to Denver! Whatever her sister had summoned her for, she couldn't have timed it better. He was no believer of miracles, but perhaps he should reconsider his attitude toward them.

"Can anyone think of anything else we have to attend to?" asked Father Dunphy.

"Nothing I can see," said Rev. Miller. "Bishop, did you know that when the bank closed today Henrietta reported that ticket sales have gone over the half-million mark? Isn't that fabulous? Four hundred fifty-nine thousand dollars on hand. We allotted ten percent for promotional expenses, and it appears they'll only come to a fraction of that, closer to two percent, according to Henrietta. And the total of prize monies will be under two hundred thousand."

"Faith," said Father Dunphy. "I hope and pray it'll all come off as smoothly as it promises to." He turned his glance on the bishop. "I hope it's as clean as the hound's tooth you mentioned when you came up with the idea."

"And why wouldn't it be, Patrick?"

"I'm only saying. Let me put it this way: if it turns out there's any tampering with the results, any hanky-panky from any quarter, I for one will be very very angry."

"I'll be outraged," said Rev. Grier. "And when I find out who's responsible, I'll see to it that he or they are drawn and quartered. Bless my soul if I don't."

"Amen," said Rev. Hollings.

He too was staring at the bishop, as were all four.

"If there's even a grain of possibility in what you suggest, I say the time to root it out is right now," said the bishop, "before the drawing."

"I didn't say there *was* any chicanery," said Father Dunphy, "merely that I hope and pray there isn't any."

"That's what he said," Rev Grier said.

"I'll go further than drawn and quartered," said Rev. Miller. "If it should turn out there's a nettle in the soup, whoever's responsible may very well not get out of Fodder City alive."

Father Dunphy sucked in his breath sharply. Rev. Grier, Rev. Hollings, and the bishop looked properly startled.

"All I'm saying is, I know a few in my flock I'd be hard put to keep from taking matters into their own hands," Rev. Miller said.

"Gentlemen, gentlemen," said the bishop, "I'm sure your fears are groundless."

"Hopefully," Rev Miller said, "but all of us here except you, Bishop . . ." He paused to sip his coffee.

The bishop gaped at him; he held his breath. Rev. Miller wiped his mouth with his napkin and went on.

"Remember James Monroe Pattee and the Wyoming lottery. Ever hear of James Monroe Pattee, Bishop?"

"Can't say that I have."

"He traveled around organizing and directing a whole series of lotteries, of which the Wyoming lottery was just one, but the biggest. The newspapers warned the population against him everywhere he went, but he still managed to carry on. They say he had five or six lotteries going at the same time by using pseudonyms and front men."

"I was once introduced to him," said Rev. Grier. "Quite an impressive fellow. Looked something like you, Bishop. Same color and style hair, but he wore a full beard as black as night. I agree with Cletus, I shudder to think James Monroe Pattee might be lurking in the wings preparing to pounce."

"Pattee or any other swindler," said Rev. Miller.

"I'm sure we have no such worry," said the bishop. "Shall we order dessert?"

* * *

It was seven-thirty when Bishop Winfield knocked at Horne's door, an hour and a half to go before the drawing. The townspeople were already gathering around the large platform festooned with banners and bunting erected in the center of Main Street. A large sign above the platform proclaimed:

Drawing Tonight!
The Grand Lottery of Crook County
Grand Prize: $100,000
Plus Many, Many Additional Prizes
Buy Your Ticket and Win Your Fortune!

The B.P.O. Elks concert and marching band would be occupying the three rows of chairs on the stand behind the dais and the barrels containing the ticket stubs. Preliminary festivities included a concert solo, a rendition of the aria "Ah fors'è lui" from Verdi's *La Traviata* by the Congregational church choir's leading soprano, a display of trick shooting, and more.

Horne answered his door. In sailed Perry.

"T.G., my boy, you'll never guess what's happened. We're in luck. What am I saying, luck, it's a miracle."

"Calm down."

"Henrietta Lacklund—she's left town, she won't be here for the drawing; more important, she won't be at the bank tomorrow morning to pay off the winners! The job is yours. She's out, you're in! Is that a miracle or not?"

"It's nothing of the sort," Horne said, his tone and expression as blasé as he could make them. "She didn't 'leave' town; she was called away by her sister down in Denver."

"How do you know that?"

"I know she has a sister, something I can't imagine you bothered to find out, but then of course you don't work with her every day. We've become good friends, Henrietta and I. She's told me all about her family. She's particularly fond of her younger sister Emily in Denver. I offered the Western Union clerk ten dollars to contact his fellow operator down there and have him send a fake telegram. I made sure it was carefully worded; I didn't want to alarm Henrietta, just get her to stir her stumps and run off to Denver. I didn't make it a matter of life and death, just please come as soon as you can. I need you. And the word desperately in front of her name at the bottom."

"You . . . paid . . . ten dollars ."

"Actually, twenty: ten for the man here in town and ten for his friend down in Denver. I'll be honest, Perry, I was beginning to get a little bit anxious. Here it is Friday and she's still on the job. I didn't know what you had in mind to get rid of her, but I didn't want to take any chances. You understand."

"I do."

"You're sore."

"I'm not; it was very clever of you, very resourceful."

"You're not sore."

"I said I'm not."

"You're jealous."

"Don't be absurd. You might have told me what you were up to."

"I planned to. What's the difference? It worked, that's all that matters. It accomplishes our purpose and you won't have to poison her husband."

"I had no intention of poisoning him."

"All we have to do now is get me assigned to take her place."

"I've already seen to it."

Horne gaped. "You have? How on earth did you know she wouldn't be here?"

"Never mind. It's settled, why discuss it further? Something else has come up."

"Prunella! I knew it! She's boozed herself into a stupor, hasn't she?"

"She most certainly has not! Last I saw of her she was dead-sober."

"Don't you think you ought to stick close to her and make sure she stays that way? The witching hour is right around the corner."

"She gave me her solemn word. Would she deliberately mess up a paying job? She wouldn't; she won't. Have you ever heard of James Monroe Pattee?"

"Who hasn't? The Lottery King."

Perry recounted the conversation at the dinner table. "If something happens, if there should be a slipup, we're going to be in big trouble."

"Are you trying to say you didn't think there'd be risk in a scam this size, this complicated? Perry, how can there not be?"

"I just never imagined it would get as big as it has. They've sold a wagonload of tickets."

"And that surprises you? There's a lot of money around here, and people love lotteries."

"They were all staring at me at the table talking about Pattee. I'm beginning to think they're a lot sharper than I've been giving them credit for. If anything goes wrong, they'll nail me to the wall."

"Relax. What can go wrong? I'll take care of my end tomorrow morning. You keep an eye on your friend Prunella tonight. Perry, do me a favor, get over to the Meadowlark and check on her. Right now. If she's squiffy, we still have an hour and three-quarters to sober her up."

"All right, all right."

"And give me our winning tickets. From now on we won't be seeing each other until we leave town."

"Wrong. We have to meet once more. I have to give you the winning stubs Prunella palms. So that when you show up at the bank in the morning you'll have our winning tickets *and* their stubs on you."

"After the drawing, slip the stubs under my door."

"Will do."

4

Perry could scarcely conceal his immense relief when Prunella answered his knock and opened the door to reveal herself cold-sober. She was dressed in a figure-flattering Eaton-style suit of navy serge cheviot, the outer jacket trimmed all around with black mohair and silk. It was five minutes to eight.

"You look positively ravishing, my dear!"

"Come in, come in."

"Magnificent. Oh, before I forget, here are the four stubs you'll be 'drawing' for us."

"The grand prize . . ."

"One hundred thousand. One ten-thousand and two five-thousand. A hundred and twenty thousand in all."

"I understand they've sold over half a million tickets."

"They have, they have. I must confess the whole business has exceeded my wildest dreams by a wide margin."

"How many winning tickets are there in all?"

"Sixty-one. Fifty one-hundred-dollar tickets, five five-thousand, five ten-thousand."

"With the grand prize, that's a hundred and eighty thousand. How come you're only chiseling a hundred and twenty?"

"I don't like that word. To answer your question, however, let me say I've given this a great deal of thought. I refuse to be tempted by greed. My dear, you know what the trouble is with people like us? We have the skills, the know-how, and the grit to work the biggest scam, the most complex, the most lucrative, but we only work whatever it is one time, then move on. We do all the preliminary work, make all the local connections we need, bring it off, pocket our money, and run. It shouldn't have to be that way."

"What way should it be?"

"We should be able to come back here six months from now and be welcomed with open arms and invited to stage another lottery. Imagine how much easier the second time around would be; using all the connections we've made in town, we could practically sit in a rocker and do the job.

"Why take only two-thirds when we can have it all?" He tapped his temple and winked. "I'm being shrewd, I'm looking down the road into the future. That's the whole trouble with our breed: we think only of the moment, not the day after tomorrow."

"I don't see how that's possible. You set a fire in any town, you have to get out before you get burned."

"The key is not to set too big a fire. Don't be greedy. The winning numbers will be selected in reverse order, the fifty hundred-dollar winners first. By the time you get to the five thousand-dollar winners the crowd will be practically bursting with excitement. You'll call the first three and they'll roar after every name. You call the fourth and fifth, ours, and they'll still roar."

"Force of habit."

"Something like that. Even though the name is a phony, somebody they've never even heard of. The same will hold true when you call out the ten thousand-dollar names. Ours will be last. Then will come a trenchant pause and *voilà*, the golden moment is upon us! The grand-prize winner is . . .

"All we'll be doing is coasting on the enthusiasm of the crowd. The cheering will be just as loud for our names as the legitimate names. But it won't be if we hog all eleven big prizes."

"I suppose it makes sense."

"More than makes sense, my dear, it's our surest protection against being found out." He checked his watch. "It's just past eight. The torchlight parade is scheduled to begin at eight-twenty. At twenty-five-to-nine everyone will be gathered around the platform and the cornet player and the singers will take over."

"Who'll be doing the announcing?"

"Reverend Miller. He'll introduce you. Give yourself ten minutes leeway; come down and join us at ten-of-nine."

"Okay. Anything else?"

"Nothing. Any questions?"

"No. Oh, there is one little thing. I'll be leaving town tonight right after the drawing. I've got a buggy waiting for me. I have to get back to Cheyenne. I'd appreciate it if you paid me now." She held out her hand.

"Of course."

He handed her a hundred dollars. Her hand remained extended.

"Five hundred, Perry."

"What?"

"Five."

"We agreed on a hundred."

"I know, but I've changed my mind. A woman's prerogative."

"This is blackmail!"

"That's an ugly word. To me it's business. Five hundred or get somebody else."

"The devil with you, I will!"

"Suit yourself. Here, take back your ticket stubs."

"Bet your boots I will!" He snatched them from her. He was suddenly trembling with rage. He seethed and fumed and scowled at her, then swung about and stomped out the door, slamming it in his wake.

The nerve, he thought, the almighty gall! Of all the double-dealing, dirty, deceitful, conniving . . . She'd planned this all along. Blackmail! Extortion!

"I never trusted her, never. T.G. was right, you can't trust a drunk!"

He had walked six paces down the hallway. He stopped. As irate as he was, as shocked and disgusted, he could not close his mind completely to concentrate on her. A narrow slit still remained through which common sense squeezed itself.

It was past eight; the drawing would begin promptly at nine. How could he possibly get someone to replace her on such short notice? He couldn't do it himself, he couldn't draft T.G. Who, then?

"There must be somebody, there's got to be!"

He thought and thought; there was no one.

"Damnation one and indivisible!"

Slowly, with the greatest reluctance, he turned and made his way back to her door. He raised his fist and knocked. The door opened so quickly she had to have been standing just inside. Opened six inches. Out came her hand. Not a sound passed between them. Her fingers motioned in request. He silently counted out five hundred dollars and lay the four stubs on it. She drew in her hand and closed the door.

He was still furious when he mounted the platform and took his chair beside Rev. Miller. The chair on the other side of him was reserved for her. He made a mental note, a warning to himself not to glare at her when she arrived.

The torchlight parade had begun early, the band leading the marchers, Mayor Mulhall's fourteen-year-old daughter, Wanda Charlotte, leading the band, dexterously swinging her baton. Perry put the crowd at around five thousand, with more people arriving every second. He spotted Sheriff Matt Coombs, who had issued the lottery committee the license to operate. He had come over from Sundance, the county seat. He wore his badge and guns and stood with his hands on his hips looking suspiciously at everyone within view.

Perry's mind raced ahead to the actual drawing and beyond it. As in all lotteries, a handful of the legitimate winners would fail to show, but under the law would have to be informed of their good fortune and given a year to collect. Every newspaper in the territory would carry the list of winners. Among the top eleven would be the four phony names, all four destined to be paid off before anyone else.

The torchlight parade snaked through town and wound up at the stand. Rev. Miller introduced the evening's entertainment, one performer following the other's applause. The soprano from the Congregational church choir cracked badly on a few of the higher notes of Verdi's opus, but the cornetist essayed Schmeckenmeier's Concerto for Cornet in B flat flawlessly, triple-tongueing his way through one intricate passage after another and earning tumultuous applause.

Three flour barrels had been set up at the front of the stand by the railing. Into them went all the ticket stubs with their purchasers' names written on them—all the stubs except the four given Prunella by Perry.

She came rustling up, all sails set, promptly at five minutes before nine to be greeted warmly by the five clergymen, introduced to the town marshal and Mayor Mulhall, and welcomed with a stony smile by Perry. Rev. Lacklund had arrived somewhat later than the others.

"I understand Mrs. Lacklund has been called away," said Perry after shaking hands.

"I just got back from running her over to Moorcroft to catch the train. Sorry I missed the dinner meeting."

"We missed you, Hildreth."

"Amos Grier tells me Mr. Tillinghast will be substituting for Henrietta at the bank tomorrow morning. There's no possible way she can get back in time to pay the winners."

"It's all right. She'll be missed of course, but as long as he can cover for her, there's no problem."

At nine sharp a cannon located behind the bank was discharged, the blast stilling the crowd and raising Rev. Miller from his chair.

"Ladies and gentlemen, friends, neighbors, and visitors, welcome all to the drawing of the Grand Lottery of Crook County."

The crowd roared, applauded, and pressed forward. Looking down upon the upturned faces, every one wearing an expression of eager anticipation, Perry felt a surge of power in his breast. By nine o'clock tomorrow morning, T.G. and he would be well across the South Dakota border $120,000 richer, hopefully in the enviable position of being able to return to Fodder City six months hence to begin all over again.

Rev. Miller droned on.

"With us tonight to draw the winning stubs is Miss Prunella Winfield, our dear friend and benefactor Bishop Bolton Winfield's sister. Let's have a rousing round of applause for Miss Winfield."

The crowd obliged.

"You just heard me refer to the gentleman on my right, Bishop Winfield, as our dear friend and benefactor. Benefactor he is, for it was his idea to hold this lottery. And to him goes much of the credit for its popularity and scope. A round of applause for Bishop Winfield."

Encore.

"Friends, you see before me three barrels." He tilted one forward, lifting the bunting out of the way so all could see inside. "They contain the stubs, all the stubs. Miss Winfield will pluck a stub from each barrel in turn, moving right to left, right to left, right to left. Now, permit me to introduce Mayor Mulhall's lovely young daughter, Wanda Charlotte, who has kindly consented to stir the stubs for us."

Wanda Charlotte stood up, setting her baton on her chair. She was many impressions to the eye, but none of them lovely. Her legs were too thin, her eyes too large for her plain face, her hair stringy, her chin all but entirely absent, and she displayed buck teeth.

"Your baton, Wanda Charlotte," said Rev. Miller.

She set about stirring the contents of each barrel.

The time had arrived. The drawing began. Again the crowd pressed forward. Studying faces, Perry noted those whose mouths moved in silent prayer, those who bit into their lower lip and held it, men who grabbed their beards and hung on, men, women, and children who held their breaths and not a few who squeezed their eyes shut and stiffened almost to cracking. Prunella drew the fifty hundred-dollar winners swiftly and smoothly. She then paused for a glass of water before continuing.

"Now, ladies and gentlemen, friends, neighbors, and visitors, we will move on to the five-thousand-dollar winners," Rev. Miller announced.

Tension was rife, excitement ran through the crowd like electricity. The applause and cheering after each of hundred-dollar winners had grown in intensity with each succeeding name.

Prunella reached into the first barrel and drew.

"Number six one four three eight. Six one four three eight."

"I got it! I got it! I win! I win!"

A grizzled, greasy-shirted, ancient prospector pushed forward, waving his ticket triumphantly.

"Mr. Abraham Hogandyke?"

"That's me! I win!"

"Indeed you do, Mr. Hogandyke," purred Prunella.

She held up his stub for all to see, then handed it to Rev. Miller, who handed it in turn to Rev. Hollings, keeper of all the winning stubs.

"Congratulations, Abraham," boomed Rev. Miller. The crowd cheered. He gestured for silence. "Be at the bank eight o'clock tomorrow when it opens and collect your money. Again congratulations."

And so it went for the other four five-thousand-dollar winners, two of whom were palmed into the proceedings by Prunella. The five-thousand-dollar winners were followed by the five ten-thousand-dollar winners, the last of whom was sneaked into the drawing by Prunella.

The crowd fell silent. One could almost hear the flickering of the torches. Once more the cannon behind the bank let loose a blast. A snare drum rolled solemnly for fully thirty seconds. Rev. Miller cleared his throat dramatically.

"Now we come to the moment we have all been waiting for. The drawing for the grand-prize winner. One hundred thousand dollars cash to be handed over to the lucky ticket holder whose number will be drawn by Miss Winfield."

"Yayyyyy!" shouted a single voice at the rear of the crowd.

A wave of grumbling cut it short. Once more Rev. Miller raised his hands.

"Let's have it perfectly quiet. And before we draw, Wanda Charlotte, will you stir the barrel one last time." She stiffled a nervous giggle and stirred. "Miss Win— ladies and gentlemen, we must have absolute silence— Miss Winfield, will you please draw the grand-prize winner?"

Prunella rose from her chair. Her glance fell downward and her eyes came to rest on Sheriff Coombs. He was looking up at her with a puzzled expression, the face of one who seemed to be trying to remember where he'd seen her face before. She smiled, raised her eyes, and swung them to the barrel. She thrust in her hand to within two inches of the top of the pile, dropped the planted stub from her sleeve into her hand, and brought it out.

"The grand-prize winning number is . . ."

The drum rolled, the onlookers froze, the torchlights danced, the wind rose and sang, someone coughed nervously, someone else hushed him.

"Two four one eight one one!"

The crowd groaned, the crowd roared, the crowd applauded vigorously, but as with the three previous held-out tickets no one stepped forward.

"Two four one eight one one."

Still no response.

"It appears the lucky grand-prize winner is not with us," said Rev. Miller, his tone crestfallen. "Stub please, Miss Winfield." She handed it to him with an appropriate flourish. "Number two four one eight one one. Mr. Harley W. Biggs. Moorcroft. Ah-hah, that accounts for it, our lucky winner is from out of town. And evidently prevented from joining us by something or other."

"He's drunk in bed," shrilled a man.

"He's in the calaboose," bellowed another.

Rev. Miller quieted them. "Whatever has detained him, Mr. Harley W. Biggs of Moorcroft is our grand-prize winner. Congratulations, Mr. Biggs, wherever you are. Attention, everyone, Mr. Biggs will be speedily informed of his good fortune. Ladies and gentlemen, friends, neighbors, visitors all, we have come to the end of the Grand Lottery of Crook County. On behalf of the lottery committee, of which I have the honor of being a member, on behalf of the marshal, Miss Winfield, and Wanda Charlotte, I thank you all for joining us. Again, congratulations to all you lucky winners and to the rest of you, better luck next time."

Perry cringed. Rev. Miller's parting words were well-intended, he was sure, but would not have been of his choosing. For the first time in days he consciously relaxed, letting his shoulders sag, his chest cave in, and his breath issue slowly from his throat.

"Thank the Lord that's over," he whispered to Prunella beside him.

"Amen. I've got to be going. Thanks for the job, Perry, see you someday somewhere."

Off she sailed to the steps and down them to the street. The crowd, displaying what could only be termed mass disappointment, milled about. Perry followed her with his eyes. Someday somewhere for sure, he mused bitterly.

And next time the shoe would be on the other foot!

5

A line was already forming when Horne arrived at the bank at seven-thirty in the morning, spectacles in place, the four held-out tickets and their stubs in his inside pocket. The bank did not open for business until eight o'clock. He stood apart from the line reading a week-old copy of the *Cheyenne Sun* that he had retrieved from a wastebasket the day before. D. Lennox Flynn arrived at seventeen minutes before the hour and let him in. He enlisted his help in pushing the doors closed against a threatened invasion of winning ticket holders, already becoming impatient at the delay. Flynn had been apprised the night before that Mr. Tillinghast would be substituting for the absent Henrietta Lacklund, dispensing the lottery prize money.

"I hope you can get this business over with before eight-thirty," groused Flynn. "I'd sure hate to think we're going to be jammed up with this rabble all morning long. Our steady customers'll have a fit."

"I wouldn't worry. I imagine the winners'll want their money right away. I take it it's all in the vault."

"In two strongboxes." He produced two keys. "Mrs. Lacklund has separated the prize money from the rest of the proceeds. I have no idea how much you'll find."

Horne grinned. "At least a hundred and eighty thousand, I hope."

His humor was lost on Flynn. He glanced about them. "Why don't you set your table up right here by the door? Lengthwise, here in the center. They can come in one at a time, you pay them, they walk around the table and out the other side."

"What about your customers?"

"Drat. Well, they'll just have to squeeze by the best they can. Judas priest, this pesky lottery's been more trouble than it's worth."

"I'll do my best."

"Are you about finished with our books?"

"All done. I would have told you yesterday, but you'd already left."

"Everything . . . okay?"

"Perfect. Right to the penny."

"Whew, thank God. Thank God for Mrs. Lacklund, she's my right arm. I hope to hell she's back by Monday morning."

Flynn opened the vault door for him. Horne located the two strongboxes. He relieved the prize money box of the $120,000 in the highest denominations he could quickly find. He checked the contents of the other box. There looked to be roughly $300,000. The five churches had come out very well, he mused, very well indeed. All operating expenses had been paid, including a ten-dollar donation to the Elks lodge for the services of the band. Perry was out five hundred dollars plus expenses for Prunella, and most certainly would not be asking to be reimbursed at this late date. She had flown; he and Perry would be on their way soon. They planned to meet at the abandoned sawmill east of town and together head for the Dakota Territory border twelve miles farther on. They could catch a southbound train in Deadwood and be in Omaha before midnight.

He divided the $120,000 into packets half an inch thick and stuffed them in various inside pockets. Taking the strongbox with the remaining sixty thousand dollars, he went back out, closed and locked the vault door, and took his seat at the table set at right angles to the front doors. Two dozen pair of eyes ogled the prize money as he stacked it. He then got out the winning stubs given him an hour earlier by Rev. Ewart Hollings. He deftly added his four held-out stubs to their number. When he collected fifteen or twenty legitimate winning tickets and the pile began to grow, he would add his four held-out tickets to it. It was quite like palming and stacking cards, the performance going on under the very eyes of the legitimate winners without their suspecting a thing.

The tellers and other employees came straggling into work. At eight o'clock Flynn unlocked the front doors, threw them open, and was nearly bowled over by the stampede.

"Gentlemen, gentlemen, gentlemen," burst Horne, "simmer down. Let's try to do this in a civilized and orderly fashion, and not disrupt the bank's transactions."

For this Flynn beamed an appreciative smile at him.

"As you come in, keep the line to your left," said Horne, "leave room at the right for those who've been paid off to leave and customers to come in. Come in one at a time; I'll signal you. No pushing or shoving, please."

He began. The twelfth man had received his hundred dollars when a familiar figure came striding in, her jaw set, fire in her eyes.

"Henrietta!" burst Horne.

"In the flesh. What do you think you're doing?"

"I . . . why . ."

Flynn came hurrying up. "Henrietta, I thought you'd gone to Denver."

"I started out for there, more's the pity. Hildreth took me to Moorcroft to catch the train. There wasn't one until eleven-thirty. I had to sit in that filthy station cooling my heels for nearly four hours."

All eyes were on her, all ears tuned to her sputtering. Horne took advantage of the distraction and slipped his four stubs into the stub pile, his four tickets into the ticket pile.

"The train finally came in and I got aboard. I had a lot of time to think in that station, a lot more on the way to Upton. I declare, that Chicago, Burlington, and Quincy Line has to be the worst in the West, the slowest, dirtiest, most inefficiently run . . . Anyway, by the time we got over the border into Nebraska I made up my mind."

"About what?" asked Horne and Flynn as one.

"The trip, of course. Or rather wild-goose chase. With every click of the rails I got more and more suspicious. Emily's telegram. Oh, it was a call for help, all right, her name attached to it, but why, I wondered, was she so vague? Why didn't she come right out and say what the problem was? It wasn't at all like her. She dotes on specifics the way you dote on numbers, Mr. Tillinghast, Edward."

"Hey, folks, excuse me, but I got a hunnert-dollar winner here," said a slender, dour-looking man in well-worn bibs and a straw hat.

"When we stopped in Harrison, I got off. It was the dead of night, of course, but luck was with me. The telegraph operator was still on the job. I got him to wire Denver and get someone at that end to get in touch with Em, bother the hour. Two hours later back came the word. You'll never guess, she never even sent a telegram!"

"No . . ." gasped Horne, looking properly appalled.

"I don't get it," Flynn said.

"Hey, folks, I got a hunnert-dollar winner here . . ."

"It was a fake, someone rigged the whole thing to get me out of town, some idiotic practical joker."

"I don't think it's very funny," Horne said.

"Hey, folks, I got a—"

"Right with you," snapped Henrietta. The man shrank from her scowl. "If I ever get my hands on whoever did it, I'll wring his neck. Let me sit down, Mr. Tillinghast, Edward, I'll take over."

"I don't mind finishing up . . ."

His mind whirled. He'd cashed in the $120,000. Only one legitimate big winner had appeared up to the moment: the seventh or eighth ticket holder in line had won five thousand dollars.

"It's my job, my responsibility. How much have you paid out so far?"

"Hey, folks, I got a hunnert-dollar winner here."

"Ah, quite a sum . . ."

She was staring at the stack of prize money. "How can that be? There's so little left. There can't be more than sixty or seventy thousand there. Get up, let me count it. Mister, you'll get your hundred dollars in one minute. Something's very wrong here, Mr. Tillinghast, Edward. Have you paid off the grand-prize winner yet?"

"I . . ."

"You must have. Where's all the money gone?"

A shout went up outside, drawing all eyes to the door. Instant bedlam broke loose, the waiting winners scattering in every direction. A host of riders had come barreling up. They jumped down from their saddles and came rushing in, waving six-guns, shotguns, rifles . . .

"Oh, my God," groaned Horne.

Flynn threw up his hands and held them there.

6

Clay Allison of Tennessee was both a successful rancher and explosive killer. Many who came in contact with him thought him deranged; his conduct and his actions served to reenforce this opinion. Once, arriving in Cheyenne with a herd of trail cattle and an excruciatingly painful toothache, he ran straight to the nearest dentist. Unfortunately, in his haste to relieve the pain, the dentist began drilling the wrong tooth. Allison bolted from the chair, left the office, went to another dentist, and paid twenty-five dollars to have the damage corrected. When he was done, he went back to the first dentist, strapped him to his own chair, pried open his mouth, and wrenched a tooth from it. He was preparing to extract a second one but gripped the man's lip instead. The dentist's screams brought help and interrupted the extraction.

Suspicion of mental infirmity was well-grounded. When the Civil War began, Allison left the family farm near Waynesboro and enlisted in the Tennessee Light Artillery. Three months later he was given a medical discharge by Confederate Army doctors; they described him as "incapable of performing the duties of a soldier because of a blow sustained years ago. Emotional or physical excitement produces paroxysmals of a mixed character, partly epileptic and partly maniacal." Whatever his aberration, Allison was a violent man, and his history sufficiently justified the almost superstitious dread in which he was held on the frontier.

His arrival with his gang in Fodder City was timely

and was destined to be most profitable. Eight outlaws surged into the bank, six others took up their posts outside to defend against any interruption.

Horne recognized Allison at his first step through the door. There was no mistaking those dark eyes pushed deep into that pale face surrounded by an unruly mop of black hair, sideburns joining beard and scalp, ears half-hidden in the growth.

"Lady, back against the wall," he growled to Henrietta. "You"—he pointed both six-guns at Horne—"on your feet and back alongside of her. Don't nobody else move. Which o' you's in charge?"

All eyes unhesitatingly turned toward D. Lennox Flynn, who seemed to shrink under their assault.

"Open the vault," Allison snapped. "Move!"

He jammed a muzzle into Flynn's gut, doubling him, setting him grunting in pain. When he straightened, his already florid face was darkening to crimson. He hurried over and opened the vault. The outlaws attacked the interior like starving wolves a fresh deer corpse. In less than a minute every bill, every gold and silver coin was removed and packed for travel. While his men worked, Allison and one other continued to cover the helpless employees and the three winners trapped inside by the intruders. Obeying instructions, Horne stood beside Henrietta against the wall alongside the door; both kept their hands high.

"You can't get away with this," she sputtered.

Allison laughed. "We're doing okay so far."

"Scum . . ."

Horne groaned, Allison's face darkened.

"Mind your tongue, woman."

"All set here, Clay," called one of his men.

"How much?"

"Millions!"

"How much!"

"A big haul, Clay, biiiig," said another man.

"Good."

"Scum!"

Allison moved closer to her, stroking the sides of her chin with the barrel of his gun. "Didn't I say mind your tongue?"

"Brave as the dickens with those guns in your hands, aren't you?"

"Let's go, Clay."

"Right. Lower your hands, woman, and rustle your skirts, you're coming with us. We can use a purty hostage."

"No," burst Horne. Allison shifted his eyes to him, his expression puzzled. "You can't take her, she's a minister's wife. Be smart, Clay, don't make more trouble for yourself than you already have."

"He's right, Clay," said the other man, helping him cover the gathering.

"Shut up, Leland." He pondered, his eyes flicking back and forth between Henrietta and Horne. "All right, you stay, woman. You, dude, move."

Before Horne could utter a syllable in protest, his shoulder was grabbed, he was spun around and being shoved out the door.

"Don't nobody move a hair till we're outta town, else we'll come back and slaughter the lot o' you," Allison bellowed.

In ten seconds Horne found himself astride a feisty little roan mare, tossing her head, airing her mane, and ready to race.

> Annie Bowater, alias Handy Annie alias Quickhand Annie alias Nellie the Sleeve, alias Prunella Vanderhook, alias, alias. Wanted for fraud, forgery, felony, subordination of perjury, soliciting money under false pretenses, soliciting, arson, larceny, robbery, burglary, willfully and maliciously placing obstructions on a railroad track, et cetera.
>
> Wells, Fargo and Company and the Union Pacific Railroad will pay a combined reward of eighty-five hundred dollars for information leading to the arrest and conviction of the above individual. Last

seen in the vicinity of Dodge City, Kansas. Haywood Marks Junior, Sheriff, Ford County, Kansas.

"Merciful heavens!"

Rev. Miller lowered the wanted dodger handed him by Sheriff Matt Coombs. The sheriff had gone back to his home in Sundance after the lottery drawing and returned early in the morning with the dodger. He sat in Rev. Miller's study. Present also were Rev. Hollings, Rev. Lacklund, Rev. Grier, and Father Dunphy. All five sat stunned.

"I was standing smack in front of the platform last night when she was drawing the numbers," said Coombs. "I knew I'd seen that face somewheres before; I just couldn't place it, not right away. That's her all right, no mistake."

"Dear me," said Rev. Miller. "It appears we've been duped, thoroughly and completely. This is dreadful!"

"It's not that bad, Cletus," said Father Dunphy. "The lottery worked out just fine, the proceeds are safe in the vault at the bank, the winners are being paid off."

"I don't think that's altogether the point, Patrick," interposed Rev. Lacklund. "I think what's worrying Cletus, what worries me, is that all of us are linked to this . . . this evil, this confidence woman."

"Exactly," said Rev. Miller, "not to mention her confederate, Bishop Winfield. They're brother and sister."

"I doubt it," said Coombs. "Whether they are or not doesn't matter much at this stage. Gentlemen, I'm sorry to have to be the one to bring you the bad news, but I thought you should know."

"Absolutely," said Rev. Grier.

"What do we do now?" asked Rev. Lacklund.

"Winfield," exclaimed Rev. Miller, snapping his fingers.

"He's long gone," Rev. Hollings said dejectedly. "He left last night in a buggy. We passed each other going in opposite directions. He—"

The door burst wide. A boy about twelve, his hair awry, eyes wild, his voice excited and as high-pitched as a girl's, flung words at them. "Sheriff Coombs, come quick! Bank's being held up! The marshal says for you to lend a hand! Quick!"

"Merciful heavens," shrilled Rev. Miller and, clapping both hands over his face, began rocking back and forth.

Perry had left town the night before, passing Rev. Hollings in the street, exchanging greetings, and wheeling out of town, heading east. Half an hour later he drew up behind the abandoned sawmill just off the Beulah Road high in the Bear Lodge Mountains. The night was clear, the stars gleamed brightly, the moon favored the road with its pale light. The breeze sang eerily through the empty structure, and Perry anchored the horse in a grassy plot and bedded himself down under the sky out of the wind behind the main building.

He didn't relish sleeping in the open with only a paper-thin horse blanket to ward off the chill and his hat for a pillow, but he was not about to take unnecessary chances. The lottery had gone off without a hitch, as he'd expected, but returning to his hotel room and passing the night in comfort could be risky. While he slept, something might crop up to disrupt the scam, create havoc, and cast the dark shadow of suspicion over him. He couldn't imagine what could go wrong, but trouble could come from any quarter and he had no desire to be there if and when it arrived.

T.G. was scheduled to show up with the $120,000 around nine in the morning. Since the bank opened at eight, that was cutting it a trifle thin; he wouldn't worry if he was late; he could be delayed an hour or more; paying off the winners could conceivably drag on till noon, although that would be stretching it. One and all had to be as eager to get their money as T.G. was to get out of town.

All in all it had gone off like clockwork. There'd been

one or two minor scares: the overzealous ministers thrusting Henrietta into T.G.'s job of dispensing the prize money, Prunella's last-minute double cross.

"I'll never call on her again, not if I live to be a hundred," he said to the moon.

The balloon could have gone up if he, T.G., or Prunella were recognized and fingered by someone, always a possibility, wherever they traveled, whatever the scam. He knew of no outstanding wanted posters bearing either his likeness or T.G.'s. He would bet there were none of Prunella floating about the territories. Good judgment and common sense governed her every move; her only weaknesses were the bottle and Lucifer's loyal demon, greed. But now, thank the Lord, she was back in Cheyenne and out of both their lives.

"For good."

Where to tomorrow, he mused? With $120,000 in their pockets they could go anywhere. They could invite their ease for months on end. Canada might be nice. Neither of them had been over the border in four or five years, not since their trip from St. John to Prince Rupert on the Grand Trunk & Pacific Railway, three thousand miles of poker that had netted them more than thirty thousand dollars apiece.

Where had it all gone? he wondered. Both were so skilled at collecting money and so discouragingly adept at frittering it away.

"This time it'll be different."

He'd talk to T.G. like a Dutch uncle, get him to agree to salt away at least a hundred thousand. Put it in a bank in Kansas City, in some big city, where it would be safe and earn them 2 percent interest. He was not a young pup anymore; it was past time he began thinking seriously about his future and eventual retirement, forced upon him by his weary body subject to occasional visits by rheumatism and the bogy that sneaked up behind him more and more often lately to whisper reminder that he was growing old, that soon he would be unable to hold up his end of the partnership. He was seventy-two and life had been hard in every respect. Ah, but exciting, at times fascinating! Whatever the game or scam, he enjoyed it, loved it, ate it up. The lottery was a prime example: he could congratulate himself on a job superbly well done. So well, so successful for all concerned he'd have no compunctions whatsoever about returning to Fodder City in six months to organize a second such venture.

He slept.

He woke at a quarter-to-seven, the sun's glare piercing his lids, hammering his eyeballs. His horse and buggy stood where he'd left them, the horse nibbling contentedly. He too was hungry, but had nothing to eat. He whiled away the next two hours wandering about the area. The mountain complex rose out of the plains, its towers and pinnacles climbing to more than seven thousand feet at Harney Point, the erosional remnant of a giant domelike structure raised sixty million years ago. Pressures from within the earth slowly thrust up a 60-by-125 mile area some nine thousand feet. In the distance he could see the conspicuous volcanic neck of Devil's Tower. Trees grew in abundance, accounting for the presence of the mill in their midst. Why it had been abandoned he could not fathom. Western yellow pine flourished, as did mahogany, elm, and bur oak. Needlegrass and grama carpeted the slopes, hosting the delicate white, yellow, and lilac mariposa lilies, tall purple mallows, pale-blue lupines, and pink fireweeds, rising above the scorched areas where lightning had immolated the trees. Deer, elk, and bighorn sheep made their homes in the heights.

At ten-fifteen T.G. still had not shown. Not a soul had passed through the area. In spite of his earlier decision not to begin worrying until noon hour, concern anchored itself in his thoughts. Had something happened? Had there been a hitch in dispensing the prize money? Worse, a hitch in sneaking their stubs and tickets into the legitimate piles?

Had someone caught him in the act? Not Flynn, he

wasn't interested in the lottery, couldn't care less how it was run or who won. Had the members of the committee dropped by the bank to keep an eye on bank examiner Tilinghast?

"Where the devil are you, boy?" The horse raised her head and looked his way, questioningly, he imagined. "Where is he? What's going on?"

The outlaws thundered out of town west in the direction of Sundance, but halfway there Allison, in the lead, raised his arm and signaled them to double back. They skirted Fodder City at a safe distance to the north, heading in the direction of Beulah and the border of Dakota Territory. Horne was centered in the pack. So fast did they move, so spirited his horse, so willing to rap his rump and send him skyward with all the jouncing, he feared that sooner or later one or another packet of money would jump out of its pocket.

It would be all he'd need, he thought wearily, to be caught holding out on them. Mr. Crazy would blow his head off. Every so often he would turn and look back at him, leering, his eyes wild looking.

"You doing okay, hostage?"

Horne ignored him. Far to their right and now behind them lay Fodder City. By now a posse had to be out chasing, he reasoned. They'd spot the tracks, they'd see the wide turn, the doubling back. Why head west in the first place? East was so inviting, no more than twelve or fifteen miles through the mountains to the border. Once over it, their pursuers would be out of the game, unless the marshal had authority to cross over after people. In towns as close to borders as Fodder City such a license wasn't uncommon. It was an arrangement that worked both ways.

Wherever they were taking him, when they stopped, Horne's first order of business was clear. He had to get away. He couldn't imagine they'd bother to chase him; once over the border they wouldn't need him. They didn't regardless; his presence in their midst would hardly dissuade the law from attacking them if they ever caught up.

Escaping intact was one problem; the other was the fortune in his coat. It would kill him to have to hand it over; Allison would kill him if he failed to and it was somehow discovered. He'd divided the money into six packets, three each in each of his inside coat pockets. When he buttoned his coat, the lumps they created made him look like a woman. He left his coat unbuttoned, preferring to run the risk of a packet jumping out, separating, and fluttering to the ground for all to see.

"Clay," called a voice at the rear, "they're coming."

Allison looked around and past Horne. His leer faded.

"Son of a bitch. How many you make it, Leland?"

"Ten, maybe twenty. Hard to tell, they're still a good two miles back."

They rounded a wide curve, erasing sight of their pursuers for the time being. Far ahead Horne recognized the sawmill where he and Perry had held two after-hours meetings. Stark and weatherbeaten, it loomed against the morning sky.

"Get a move on, boys, make for that mill dead ahead. We'll get 'round back, hide the horses, and bushwhack 'em."

"They'll see us, Clay."

"Not if we move, goddammit!"

Perry spotted the dust cloud approaching, the small black figures beneath it. He instinctively sensed trouble. He was standing at the rear corner of the building, his horse and buggy behind him. He ran inside. The cast-iron machinery, much of it broken, suggesting that either vandals or outraged former employees had attacked it with sledgehammers, occupied most of the ground-floor area. Machinery that wasn't broken was badly rusted. Lumber bins yawned emptily, wood scraps littered the floor. A rickety-looking stairway climbed to a second-floor office wedged in one corner. There was a single large window at right angles to the door, affording whoever was in charge a panoramic view of the activity below.

He hurried up the stairs. The office was even smaller inside than it appeared to be from below. There were two chairs and a rolltop desk. A worktable was set under the window, with less than a foot of space allotted between one end and the corner of the window, presumably to allow whoever oversaw operations to stand at the corner close enough to the window to see what went on directly below.

Perry stood there, looked down, and waited. The door creaked slightly open to his left. He closed it and made sure the latch was secured. The breeze sneaked through the slits in the walls, curling up to the roof, humming mournfully. He listened. Presently the sound of hoofbeats arrived. It grew louder. He could hear the riders pulling up behind him. In they trooped, dusting off their chaps with their hats, carrying on raucously. They were heavily armed.

"Great Caesar's ghost!"

He recognized T.G. As he did so, T.G., as if feeling his eyes upon him, turned and looked upward, as did the man alongside him, who looked suspiciously like Clay Allison to Perry. Perry pulled back and flattened against the wall, wondering as he did so if either had caught a glimpse of him. His shock at seeing T.G. had delayed his reaction a split second. Long enough for Allison—and he was now certain it was he—to see him?

Whether he had or not wouldn't make much difference; they had to know somebody was there from the horse and buggy. He chanced another look down. T.G.'s captors were searching about and settling in for what looked like an ambush.

The entire picture became distressingly clear in an instant. Allison and his men had hit the Miners and Merchants Bank and had come away with T.G. as hostage and the $120,000, the churches' proceeds, and whatever else of value they could find. No sooner did he arrive at this conclusion than he heard someone coming up the stairs. He cast about, looking for something to use as a wedge to lock the latch in place. There was nothing. He grabbed it and held on tightly. To no avail. Whoever had come up elected to open the door the easy way. He stepped back, raised one leg, and kicked it in.

"Good morning," said Perry politely.

"What the hell you doing here?" Allison asked.

"I'm . . . Well, if you promise not to tell anybody . . ."

"I asked you a question, old man."

"I'm on the run from the marshal in Fodder City."

"Oh, horseshit. What the hell could a decrepit old gaffer like you do to get the law on his tail?"

Perry took an instantaneous dislike to the man. He was cut off before he could reply.

"Never mind, come on downstairs. We're just about to put on a show, and you can watch."

"Strange name for an ambush."

"Hold it just a second."

He searched Perry, found no gun, holstered his own, and marched him back downstairs. They passed Horne; the two of them looked through each other.

"This is Mr. Tilly something," Allison said. "Tilly, this is . . . What's your name, Pop?"

"None of your damned business, insolent pup."

Allison's eyes shifted back and forth between uncle and nephew. "All right, you two, we're going to have us a little fireworks. I'd advise you to get down on your bellies and stay there. Get back in the corner there."

T.G. and Perry exchanged glances and complied. Seconds later they lay prone side by side.

"What in the world happened?" Perry asked.

"Sssssh."

The shooting started, the ambushers letting loose a withering barrage. Horne and Perry couldn't see a thing, but could hear and easily picture the devastating effect of the first wave of gunfire. Horses neighed and whinnied, men shouted and cursed, lead came flying at the mill so heavily it threatened to topple it. It gouged through the rotten siding, it sneaked through openings. Two men were killed instantly, a third rolled around in agony, clutching his head before expiring.

"Jesus Christ," Allison boomed. "They're loaded for bear."

"They outnumber us, Clay. Two to one."

"Who cares, Elon? We got the edge, got the cover."

"Some cov—"

He never finished; he took a slug squarely in one eye, widened the other, gaped, and gasped his last before toppling on his face.

Horne began to inch forward on his belly.

"Where do you think you're going?" Perry rasped.

"I want to see."

"Don't be an idiot, get back here."

Horne turned and came back to him. Perry stared down his chest; his coat was unbuttoned.

"The money!"

"Sssssh, they don't know."

"Give it to me."

"What for?"

"If they search you, they'll find it and kill you for holding out on them."

"They haven't searched me yet."

"They haven't had a chance, they've been on the move since Fodder City. Use your head, T.G., they'll never suspect I'm carrying it. Besides, they've already searched me. And my coat's bulkier than yours."

"All right, all right."

Horne sat up and, with his back to the outlaws, passed him the six packets. The last one had no sooner disappeared into Perry's coat when Horne, still facing the rear of the building, looked past him and spotted smoke curling up in three places.

"Allison . . ."

The leader ignored him.

One of his men got his attention. "They're not

wearing badges, Clay, nary a one I can see. What do you think?"

"They got to be the law, just ain't got their tin on."

"Allison!"

"What do you want, Tilly? Can't you see we're busy."

"Can't *you* see they're setting fire to the place."

"He's right, Clay."

"We gotta get outta here," Leland said. "Let me take a look out the back door."

Allison scowled. "Don't you dare. You show yourself, they'll fill you so fulla lead you'll need twenty pall-bearers."

Smoke was rapidly filling the place. The crackling of flames could be heard, though as yet no flames could be seen inside. Smoke began pouring through both side walls as well as the rear.

"We're trapped," bawled Leland. He was a good foot taller than Allison, broader, rangier, and Horne could see that the leader favored him. He appeared to be his second in command; at the moment, however, he was beginning to come apart. "What do we do, Clay?"

Allison cast about. All eyes were on him. "Fetch the saddlebags with the money . . ."

"I ain't showin' my face out back," exclaimed a heavy-set man, his rifle smoking in his hand.

Allison glared. "Shut up, Moss, nobody's telling you to. How many you see out there, Lefty?"

A man kneeling by a two-inch crack at the front peered through it. "Only three . . . no, four. Last minute or so they been movin' . . ."

"Around back," said Allison. "We'll go out the side and around front. While they're standing out back waiting, we'll grab their horses and make a run for it."

"They'll hear us," Moss said.

"By the time they do we'll be mounted and moving. So they'll take our horses; I know these hills, we can shake 'em easy."

"Don't try it," Horne said.

"Shut up, Tilly!"

"It's a trap."

"Trap's out back, mister, any fool can see that. I know what I'm doin', I always know. Leland, Moss, everybody except you two boys at the front, let's go. You boys keep firing till we're outside and can cut them bastards down, then you come out. Make it fast, everybody, faster than you've ever run in your lives. Their horses are up back of the boulders. Make a beeline for 'em."

"Don't do it," Horne repeated.

Three of the men glanced at him fearfully, then at Allison, but he ignored him. By now the fire had taken hold in earnest. The mill was as dry as tinder; in seconds it would be an inferno. Back, side, or front, they had to get out.

The attackers outside had taken up positions behind a convenient scattering of boulders, making it difficult to get a bead on them. Allison and his men may have been hidden targets, but the attackers' heavy fire, kept chest-high, was taking out one defender after another, bullets slamming through the plank siding as easily as if it had been tissue paper. Six outlaws were already dead and two mortally wounded, leaving Allison with only five survivors. Two held their positions at the front as ordered; the others, pushing Perry and Horne ahead of them, ran out the side door, Allison bringing up the rear.

The two defenders left behind temporarily threw a barrage at the attackers, so heavy and so well-sustained they were forced to pull back behind their cover, allowing the escapees to gain the road and cross it almost to within reach of the boulders. The majority of attackers who had moved to the rear of the building were caught off-guard by the maneuver. Billowing smoke and flames obscured their view down the side and they did not react until the two men left inside gave it up and rushed out the door. Both were cut down before they reached the corner of the building. Another was felled crossing the road, taking five shots in the back and dropping into the rain ditch, but Leland and Moss reached cover, as did Allison. Their hostages, unarmed, hanging on to their hats with both hands as they ran, drew no fire, much to the relief of both.

Allison and his men mounted up and were moving out before the attackers positioned behind the boulders turned to fire on them. Moss was hit and tumbled from his saddle, Leland grabbing his saddlebags as he fell. He and Allison got clear.

Perry and Horne never reached the horses.

"Stand where you are," roared a voice behind them.

A single shot whistled between their heads to underscore the order. They froze in their tracks and raised their hands.

"So near and yet so far," Perry murmured.

The other attackers quickly surrounded them. The outlaw who'd noted that none of them wore badges had been right, mused Horne; there wasn't a star in the bunch. The last to join the circle was a woman. She was dressed in a mule-skinner's fringed buckskins, a wide-brimmed black stetson, man's boots, and wore twin ivory-grip Peacemakers. Her attire and her guns were a shock to both Perry and Horne.

Her face provided even more of a shock.

"Prunella . . ." gasped Perry.

7

Prunella surveyed Perry with a critical eye, completely ignoring Horne standing beside him.

"Where's he heading?" she asked.

"Allison? How should I know? Either of us. You think he'd make us party to his plans?"

"You were with him long enough. He must have said something."

"He said nothing," said Horne. "What are you doing here?"

"I'm asking the questions."

"She obviously had every intention of robbing the robbers," Perry rasped petulantly. "You should be ashamed of yourself, Prunella; you have to be the greediest human I have ever had the dubious pleasure of meeting."

"Listen to him, boys," she said, "the pot calling the kettle black. Pericles, for old time's sake I'll explain."

"No need," said Perry. "We'd both have to be deaf, dumb, and blind not to be able to figure it out. You left Fodder City last night, connected with your band of merry men here, whiled away the night somewhere out of town, though not too far out, and bright and early came running back to hold up the bank. Only not early enough . . ."

"How clever of you."

"I'm a clever fellow."

"You're also dead wrong."

"You had a working agreement with Allison," Horne said, "only he double-crossed you."

"That's close. I ask you again, Perry, and I want a straight answer. Where is he heading?"

"I tell you we don't know. We were his hostages, not his confidantes."

"What are we standing around palavering for?" asked a tough-looking man with a livid scar running straight down from his left eye. "All the while they're getting farther and farther—"

"Do you know these mountains, Mr. Hobbs?" Prunella asked.

"I . . ."

"Neither do I, nor any of us. If you remember, we settled that before the first shot was fired. We could ride around in circles the rest of the day, exhaust the horses and ourselves looking for them, and be no better off than we are this minute. Logic suggests they're heading for the border. The question is, where will they light when they're safely across it?"

"Deadwood," said another man.

Prunella scratched her cheek and knit her brows. "I wonder. It's the first place he'd think we'd think of. They could just as easily head for Bellefource or Sturgis."

"Or New Yawk City," muttered Hobbs. "We're sure 'nough giving 'em time enough to get wherever they please."

"We'll head for Deadwood," Prunella said. The men grumbled in reaction. "Deadwood because he may think our first thought will be there, that we'll reject it because it's the most obvious destination, and he'll be safe there."

"That's pretty flimsy," said Hobbs, "if you don't mind my saying so."

"Say what you please, Mr. Hobbs."

"I will. I can't speak for the rest o' you, but far's I'm concerned the job's over. You hired us to catch him, we did."

"Only he got away," Prunella interposed.

"That's not my fault," responded Hobbs.

"It's not mine. Mr. Hobbs, the job's not over till I say it is."

"I'm going home." He stuck out his hand. "I'll take my hundred bucks like we agreed on."

Prunella shook her head, set her jaw, and fired her eyes at him. "You're not listening, you don't get a red cent till we get him."

"Listen here, woman . . ."

Out snaked both her six-guns. "Get on your horse and get out of here."

"You're making a mistake. There's eleven of us, eleven against one . . . three."

"Count us out," said Perry. "We want no part of a family squabble."

"There's no squabble," said Prunella evenly. "The rest of you, ride with me two more days, just two, and I'll double your money. Whether we catch up with him or not. Is it a deal?"

It was.

Hobbs' eyes traveled from face to face; they landed on Prunella's, and he smiled sheepishly at her. "Sounds fair to me."

"It's not meant for you, Mr. Hobbs. You're out, get out of here."

"Riders coming," said a short, bowlegged man whose gun belt needed tightening two notches.

"Good-bye, Hobbs."

He put on an expression of pure hatred, but said nothing further, got on his horse, and rode off, passing the approaching posse.

'What's going on here?" asked the sheriff. "Looks like old home week."

With him were the marshal and ten deputies. All were covered with dust, all looked weary and decidedly short of patience. Failure set every face with the grimness of a mourner. Perry launched into an explanation. If Sheriff Coombs heard him, he gave no sign. His wandering eyes had come to rest on Prunella.

"Annie Bowater!" he snapped, cutting Perry off between syllables. "As I live and breathe." Up came his hand, pointing at Prunella. "You're under arrest."

"I beg your pardon. Did I hear you say Annie Bowater? Dear me, not again. It's so annoying. It's come to be the cross I bear. We, Annie and I, bear a remarkable resemblance to each other. Time and again I've been mistaken for her, but I can assure you, I'm not she. My name is—"

"Turn it off, would you please? You're her, all right. I got a list of charges against you long enough to cover your whole family. You've been up to your old tricks back in Fodder City, I see. Marshal, she's all yours."

"This is an outrage."

The sheriff dismissed her with a wave and turned to Perry. "Your face is familiar too, friend. It just doesn't go with your duds. What's your name?"

"Marblehall. I was kidnapped by Clay Allison and his gang. The classic innocent bystander, that's me."

"Don't believe a word the old coot says," Prunella flared. "His real name's Perry Youngquist. I've known him thirty years. He's a professional gambler and con artist. He rigged the lottery in Fodder City."

"She's confused, poor woman . . ." began Perry. "A touch of the sun, perhaps."

"It's him, all right, Matt," said the marshal to Sheriff Coombs. "Only without the hard collar and preacher getup. The bishop . . ."

A number of the deputies agreed.

"Running a scam, were you? Okay, we'll take you in, too. And who are you?"

"My name is Edward Tillinghast," Horne said.

"His name's Horne," burst Prunella. "He was in on it, too. He's a tinhorn gambler, partners with the old man here."

"She really must be suffering sunstroke," Perry said. "This gentleman and I met for the first time this week. Mr. Flynn at the bank introduced us. He is who he says he is, Sheriff, Edward Tillinghast. Word of honor."

"Liar," yelled Prunella.

"That's Tillinghast, all right," the marshal said. "Bank examiner. He's been examining the books all week long." Horne sighed in relief and flashed a glance at Perry, whose eyes were hard at work drilling Prunella mercilessly.

"What you doing mixed up in this, mister?" the sheriff asked.

"I was taken hostage by Allison and his men."

"Where are they now?"

"They got away from this bunch." He pointed off. "By now they must be over the border. Only two of them, though; the rest were killed."

Coombs surveyed the area. "Place looks like Bull Run the day after." He looked Horne up and down. "Okay, Mr Tillinghast, you're free to go. You coming back with us to Fodder City?"

"No, thank you, the Gilmer and Salisbury stage will be coming back through, heading for Cheyenne. My next assignment is the bank in Newcastle. I should be able to get there by late afternoon."

"Suit yourself. The rest of you boys get out of here. I can't be bothered sorting out this massacre. Annie, Bishop Whoever-you-are, get on your horses, we're taking you in."

"What about the lottery money?" asked the marshal. "There's three or four hundred thousand—"

The sheriff shook his head. "I'm sorry, Wardell, they've got to be out of the county by now, out of my jurisdiction. If they come back into Crook, I'll pick up the chase. Till they do, it's in somebody else's lap."

"The preachers are going to raise hell when they hear this. The whole town'll hit the ceiling."

"I'm sorry, all I can do is get the word on the wire."

"I know, I know . . ." The marshal glanced at Prunella, then at Perry. "I'll do what I can to keep you two from being strung up, but I'm not making any rash promises. Let's go."

Perry cast one last glance at Horne. His eyes spoke:

You're on your own, my boy. Horne caught himself just as he was about to nod that he understood. On his own, he ruefully agreed. To do what? Chase Allison for the lottery money? The prize money, the $120,000 held out that he'd given to Perry, that he was carrying at the moment, suddenly looked to be as lost as the proceeds in Allison's saddlebags.

It occurred to him that if he hadn't yielded to Perry's demand that he pass it to him for saferkeeping, he'd be riding away with it intact, and the devil take Clay Allison, Leland, Prunella, Fodder City . . .

Whatever you do, Perry, don't unbutton your coat. Sleep in it, sit in jail in it, go to court in it, but don't, whatever you do, take it off!

8

If anybody in the world was more conscious of and concerned with the money in the coat than was Horne, it was the wearer. Each of the six packets suddenly felt like a gold brick to Perry as he climbed into the buggy and followed Prunella on her horse down the road in the direction of Fodder City just in front of the marshal.

Perry walked into his cell and heard the key turn in the lock without a murmur. It wasn't until Prunella was safely locked in a cell opposite that he found his voice.

"I shall never forget you for this, my dear."

She sniffed. "Just shut up."

"Dear me, how can you be so quick to recommend that which you decline to do yourself? You must feel very proud. Out of the kindness of my generous heart, of all the lovely ladies I know whose capabilities vastly exceed your own—and their number is legion—I select you. I cooperate with you in every way, I lavish praise on you unstintingly in front of the committee members, I submit to your eleventh-hour demand for five hundred dollars, outrageously unfair though it may be, and pay you before you so much as lift a finger. I give you my thanks and my blessing, and this is what I get for them: treachery, deceit, betrayal. The proverbial viper in the womb couldn't begin to hold a candle to you."

"A girl has to protect herself."

"You didn't have to tattle on me. It would have been no skin off your nose if you'd let me walk away without blabbing. I could have talked my way out of it."

"Don't be a ninny. The sheriff had you pegged the

first time he looked at you. The only thing that threw him was your clothes, and for only a few seconds. The marshal and all of his men recognized you. What do you expect, sitting up on the stand last night in full view of everybody and his brother?"

"You conveniently overlook one thing, my dear: I'm as guiltless as a lamb."

"Ha!"

"I am. Think about it."

The inner door opened. It was the marshal. Behind him came Rev. Miller and Rev. Grier.

"Gentlemen to see you, Bishop . . . Mr.—"

"Youngquist," Prunella said. "Youngquist. It's Swedish."

"Bolton . . ." began Rev. Miller, his tone sorrowful.

"Cletus . . . Marshal, would it be possible for me to speak with these gentlemen outside?" He looked straight at Prunella. "In privacy?"

"I suppose, if you give me your word you won't try anything."

"My word of honor."

"Ha!" boomed Prunella. "You're taking a big chance with him, Marshal. He's slick as an eel. Make doubly sure the shotgun rack is locked up. And don't stand near him gun side to."

Rev. Lacklund, Rev. Hollings and Father Dunphy came in as the marshal, Perry, and his other visitors emerged. The marshal locked the inner door behind them.

"That one sure is a fireball," he said.

"She's the devil in corsets!"

Chairs were set out for the five visitors.

"I got to go across the street for something to eat," the marshal said. "I'm putting you on your honor not to try nothing. I'll be right across the way the whole time with my eye on this place. You can't get out the back way and I'll see you if you try the front. You try, and by Judas, I'll shoot you first and ask you why you did after, savvy?"

"You needn't worry, I'll be here when you get back. By the way, I haven't had a morsel of food since last night. I'm absolutely famished. Could you bring me something back?"

He reached into his inside coat pocket. His fingers touched a twenty-thousand-dollar packet. He recoiled as if they'd touched fire. He got out his wallet.

"That's okay. It's on the town. All prisoners' meals are. How's about a ham-and-cheese sandwich?"

"Anything, thank you. No mustard."

All five waited until the front door closed behind the marshal. Then all five began talking at once. Perry raised his hands and they fell silent. The hurt in their eyes touched him, and for the first time in a long time shame seeped out of his conscience and into his heart.

"Gentlemen, gentlemen, may I please be the first to speak? Thank you. Let us examine what we have here. I come to Fodder City in the guise of Bishop Bolton Winfield. You accept me at face value. I propose we get up a lottery to raise money for your churches. I help in every way, even to bringing to town an old and very dear friend to assist us. Remember, it wasn't my idea to ask her to draw the tickets."

"It was mine," Rev. Grier said.

"It was all of ours," Rev. Miller said.

"Nor was it my idea to take charge of the overall operation," said Perry. They nodded. "The tickets were sold, the proceeds going into the special account which, Reverend Lacklund, Mrs. Lacklund, was in charge of. Every penny was accounted for. Not a penny ended up in my pockets." He paused; he could feel his cheeks tingling slightly; he hoped it didn't show. "Every penny went into the bank. The night of the drawing the winning tickets were drawn in full view of everyone, including the marshal and Sheriff Coombs, including all of us. So far, what has been nefarious, what criminal, what have I or anyone done that's tainted with the slightest suspicion? Not a blessed thing, gentlemen.

"The sixty-one prize winners were picked and the

next morning assembled at the bank to receive their money. Along comes this Allison person with his small army of desperadoes to empty out the bank. Off they ride, taking poor Mr. Tillinghast with them."

"Did you know that he spoke up for Henrietta?" said Rev. Lacklund. "Told them straight out she was a minister's wife. They took him instead. The man's a bonafide hero. What became of him, I wonder?"

"If he's still alive," Perry said gravely, "let us all hope and pray he's gotten away from those savages. I understand Allison is mentally deranged; a man like that wouldn't hesitate to blow poor Mr. Tillinghast's head off at the slightest provocation.

"Gentlemen, have I made my point or not? Your lottery was on the up and up from beginning to end—that is, from beginning to this morning, when the outlaws intruded. In every respect I stand before you as guiltless as a lamb, as innocent of any wrongdoing as any one of you."

"You told us your 'old and very dear friend,' the Bowater woman, was your sister," said Father Dunphy.

Perry cringed inwardly. Slip of the tongue.

"She is . . ."

"Make up your mind."

"Sister, of course. And, it appears, my cross to bear. If anyone can be fairly blamed for another's indiscretions, then blame me."

"She didn't do anything," said Rev. Miller to Father Dunphy. "Besides, no man is his brother's keeper. Or sister's."

"Nevertheless," Rev. Grier said, "your sister does have something of a shaded history. Sheriff Coombs told us there are at least a dozen charges outstanding against her. He showed us her wanted poster."

"All of which comes as much of a shock to me as it does to you," Perry said. "Had he shown it to me, I would have wept on the spot. Speaking of charges, what are yours against me, specifically?"

Rev. Lacklund reacted aghast. "Charges?"

"We've brought no charges," said Rev. Miller. "We only wanted to talk to you. To be sure, there are some loose ends."

"Such as?"

"Why did you come to town posing as a bishop, of all things?"

"Had I come as an ordinary individual, would you have listened to me?"

"Why come at all?" Rev. Miller asked.

"Why, indeed?" He glanced from one face to the next. Skepticism was creeping into every expression. He was suddenly on thin ice with not a rope in sight. "Would you believe me if I told you I came purely out of altruism, that one arrives at a point in one's life when one realizes one has to make . . . amends. One who has led the sort of life I've led can't reach my age without misgivings, without looking back over one's career and recalling too many things that trouble one's conscience and deeply, things that stir regret.

"There's a higher authority that every one of us must one day answer to. When I stand before my maker . . ."

Rev. Grier groaned; Rev. Lacklund hung his head; Father Dunphy raised his eyes, suggesting supplication to the Almighty; Rev. Hollings shook his head; Rev. Miller rose slowly from his chair.

"It's time we were going, Mr. Youngquist." He was suddenly ice-cold; his words came hollowly from his throat; he leaned too close to Perry. "I don't know what you've done or how you managed it; all the same I can't help feeling like a sheep that's been shorn." The others nodded; they too were staring coldly. "I've a very uncomfortable feeling, Mr. Youngquist. I don't like it, and I hold you responsible for it. If you've done nothing at all—and I don't for a moment believe that—you've made all five of us feel like fools, and look like fools in the eyes of our people. You lied about Annie Bowater, Lord knows what else you've lied about.

"Perhaps someday we'll get at the truth of it, not your version, but what actually happened here after you so cleverly pulled the wool over our eyes. Good day to you, sir, and may God have mercy on your conscience."

"Good day," Perry mumbled. He couldn't think of anything to add. As they filed out, the marshal came back in.

"I'm going to have to put you back in your cell now."

"Mmmmmm."

"Something the matter?"

"Not a thing."

"They were out of ham. I got you roast beef. No mustard."

"Marshal, what's the charge against me?"

"Good question."

"You can't hold me without a charge."

"How's suspicion of rigging the Great Crook County Lottery sound? Sounds okay to me. Here's your grub. On your feet."

Perry got up; he could feel the money in his pockets pressing against his chest. He could see them walking together toward the restaurant across the street, their heads down, none of them talking. He was tempted to run to the door, call them back, and give them the money, all of it, rid himself of it once and for all, but he could not.

It wasn't theirs. It wasn't his. It wasn't anybody's.

9

Horne could think of two valid reasons to chase after Clay Allison and Leland: to recover the lion's share of the money and thereby get Perry off the hook; and to see the deranged one behind bars, where he belonged, to prevent his spilling any more blood—a public service that couldn't help but win him praise in high circles and low.

He could think of one reason not to go after him: he could wind up getting his head blown off. Allison and Leland would recognize him on sight and wouldn't hesitate to shoot. As for Perry, whatever the dilemma, he could take care of himself. He could talk his way out of a Mexican firing squad. True, he'd hoodwinked the town clergy and everybody else and made them look like gullible ninnies, but he hadn't taken a penny of their monies. Actually, they had no charge that would stick. The only real culprit in the picture was Allison. As matters stood, they'd probably wind up running Perry out of town with a warning never to show his face there again.

Still, if somebody got the bright idea to search him . . .

Horne poured himself another glass of bourbon and sipped it slowly: lubrication for the wheels of his mind. As a rule, he never drank the hard stuff, preferring a decent French brandy or wine, but the job confronting him demanded stronger fortification, besides which, bourbon was speedier and more effective at chasing his fatigue and relaxing him. He sat by himself at a table in the Green Front Sporting House in Deadwood. He had caught the Gilmer–Salisbury stage as he'd told the sheriff he planned to, only the northbound one instead of the south. He had considered the situation from every conceivable angle and decided that he owed it to Perry, to all, including himself, to at least try to find Allison and Leland. Deadwood seemed their likeliest destination. Bellefource was too tame, Sturgis overrun with bluebellies, thanks to the proximity of Fort Meade. Deadwood, a jungle of false fronts, a steady flow of liquor, and more women than Sturgis and Bellefource combined, was the perfect oasis for two bank robbers loaded with cash looking to rest and enjoy themselves before returning to work.

The town consisted of one street hanging between a canyon wall and a mountain stream. One could stand in the middle of Main Street facing the hill where Boulder Canyon Road veers off toward Sturgis and see the famed Deadwood Badlands, bald rolling hills colored tan, with bands of red, pink, and brown. So steeply pitched was the terrain, vegetation seldom got a chance to establish itself on the slopes.

The town itself sat on hilly ground at an elevation of more than three-quarters of a mile, surrounded by well-worked but still-productive gold mines. Most prominent was the Homestake. The ore was low-grade, worth anywhere from two to eight dollars a ton, but there seemed no end to it, it was easily extracted and the gold liberated by stamping and amalgamation. At one time or another Deadwood hosted Calamity Jane, Wild Bill Hickock, Doc Holliday, and Wyatt Earp. Poker Alice Ivers, too, shuffled and dealt there. Theatrical stars of varying magnitude performed at the Bella Union and Gem theaters.

There were more saloons in Deadwood than all other establishments combined, and seemingly more liquor than the water that flowed through Whitewood Creek. Pistol shots outside in the street punctuated the piano player's rendition of "My Lulu, She's a Dandy." Patrons in the corner were bucking the tiger, a poker game was in progress, the place was mobbed, and the lone bartender seemed to have four hands, so busy was he, so fast did he move. He was tidily dressed in a boiled white shirt, his sleeves protected by calico cuffs, his apron white, his four-in-hand also. The only departure from his whiteness was a brocaded vest. Well-waxed handlebar mustaches spread across his genial face, his hair was parted in the middle and plastered down with either Lucky Tiger or "Prince Albert's own hair pomade." Horne had spoken briefly with him before sitting down. T.G. wisely had not asked him specifically if Clay Allison was in town; instead, he had identified himself as a roving journalist interested in making contact with Poker Alice Ivers, Wyatt Earp, or any other notables who might be in town. As far as the bartender knew, there was no one of consequence.

Horne sipped his glass down to halfway and thought again about Perry. He felt a trifle guilty for standing idly by and letting the sheriff and marshal take him away, but there was nothing he could think of that he might have done to prevent it without betraying their relationship and arousing the law's suspicions. Again he reassured himself that Perry would be able to talk himself out of the situation; he'd done so dozens of times before, at least twice he knew of, when irate mobs were preparing to string him up. This presented no such danger.

Or did it? If they looked inside his coat and found the money, there would be hell to pay. Only twelve of the sixty-one winners had been paid off before Allison and his gang arrived, only one five-thousand-dollar winner. No one else in town had gotten a penny out of the lottery. Discovery of the money in Perry's coat could make people so incensed they might very well storm the jail, haul him out, and string him up.

"My God, it could happen, it could—"

"What could happen?"

She was tall, superbly shaped, with round, full breastworks, an unblemished complexion, a pair of mischievous-looking hazel eyes, a slightly turned-up nose, a small, prettily formed mouth. Her chestnut hair was neatly bound and gathered in a net with sequins and a roll of gold tassels at the side. She wore a handsome brooch and a diamond ring that dazzled the eye. Her dress was scarlet with a gray band around the skirt.

"My name is Gilda. What's yours?"

"Alistair Richardson. Would you like to buy me a drink?"

She smiled warmly. "You're cute." She sat. "Just come to town?"

A shotgun went off in the street, the sound sharply contrasting with the pistol shots that came before and immediately after it. It brought some of the patrons to the front window.

"Just."

He got another tumbler from the waiter and filled it for her. She was just what the doctor ordered, he decided, studying her as she drank. Life had been all tension and no fun for better than a week, culminating in the hectic go-round with Allison and his friends, the ambush, the battle, the dozen near brushes with death, the uncomfortable ride on the stage. He badly needed relaxation. He could see in her eye that she liked him. It wasn't six o'clock yet, the sun was only beginning to lower over the Black Hills, but he was ready for bed. *If* Allison and Leland were in town, they'd be here awhile; if they never showed up . . . He shrugged.

"What are you shrugging for?" Gilda asked.

"If Jesse and Frank James haven't come to Deadwood, I'll just have to check around and see where they did go."

"You a lawman?"

"Journalist. I'm writing a series of articles on Western badmen for the Associated Press in New York."

"How interesting."

"This place is bedlam. Where can we go for a little privacy?"

"My place, Room Two B, the Deadwood Hotel. It's just up the street."

"Let's go."

"I can't, not yet. I won't be through work till ten o'clock. Is that too late for you?"

She'd be disappointed if he said yes. He pressed her hand and looked at her soulfuly. "Every hour will be like a year."

She laughed. "You *are* cute."

At nine-thirty he knocked on her door. She opened and smiled invitingly. She had undressed and put on a silk chiffon peignoir; the bodice failed to conceal her breasts completely.

"I'm a little early . . ." he began.

"That's okay. I got off early. Come in."

The bedroom was surprisingly tastefully furnished, not at all frilly, overdecorated, overperfumed with jasmine, lavender, or the scent of orange blossoms. There was a double bed that took up half the room. He gazed at it yearningly; he felt as though he could sleep for a week. She had other ideas.

"What's your name?" she asked.

He was puzzled; she'd asked him earlier. "Alistair Richardson."

"That's a lovely name. You're cute."

She closed on him, took hold of his arms, and put them around her. She kissed him hungrily, broke, and kissed again, this time thrusting her tongue into his mouth. He melted slightly; he could feel his member begin to stiffen. She pressed hard against him and she too felt it.

"Mmmmmm," she murmured.

He drove deep and hung on for dear life as she wrenched and bucked wildly.

"Don't move, don't move, don't move, don't move, don't move! I'm coming, coming, coming, coming, coming . . . Ahhhh!"

One last time she drove upward, then very slowly she lowered, releasing him, easing him off her. He lay back, staring at the ceiling. The door clicked open.

There she stood!

"What the . . ." He stared at her where she stood in the doorway, dressed as she was at his table in the

Green Front Sporting House; he stared at her lying beside him as naked as a newborn jay.

"Identical twins!" No wonder she didn't remember his name. "I'll be damned."

Gilda came in and introduced him to Gertrude beside him. He remained flabbergasted; both laughed gaily.

"I told you ten o'clock," Gilda said.

"I . . . came . . . early."

"I just came myself!" Gertrude laughed.

Gilda stripped to the buff with lightning speed, clearly borne of considerable practice. They prepared to go to work at the same time. It would have been impolite of him to refuse, he thought; still fear wormed through his mind. Gertrude had already proven more than he could handle. Would Gilda be just as overpowering?

Why fight it? he mused. Better to lie back and submit to every delicious depradation they had in mind. If they killed him, he'd at least die happy.

They took turns eating him, then Gilda mounted him while Gertrude hovered above his face and, lowering her breasts onto it, massaged his mouth. He'd never have believed himself capable of a fourth erection in less than thirty minutes, but erect he was. Would his heart give out before they were satisfied? Would he pass out from the strain? Would one or the other snap it off at the base?

He lasted about fifteen minutes more; fortunately, they took pity on him and ceased their assault. Gertrude poured the three of them drinks, brown liquid fire that tasted suspiciously like Valley Tan, which invariably made him sick as a dog. But not drinking would be rude, he thought, and sipped politely.

His member felt as if he'd thrust it into a pile of red-hot coals and left it there. Sitting on the edge of the bed, he looked down at it hesitantly and was surprised and elated to see it hadn't been reduced to a cinder.

"The usual fee's two dollars," Gilda said. "Three for both at the same time." He reached for his pants and his wallet. "For you, Alistair, it's on the house; right, Gertrude?"

"Right, Gilda. You're cute, Alistair."

So they liked him enough to give him a free ride; he wondered if he could trust them. He had to trust somebody in Deadwood or continue to wander around in the blind looking for Allison and Leland.

"Alistair's a journalist with the Associated Press," Gilda said. "Looking for killers and road agents and such, the big names, to write about."

"They all come to Deadwood at one time or another," Gertrude said.

He made up his mind. "What about Clay Allison?"

"Crazy Clay?" Gilda shrugged. "I don't know if he's around."

"I don't either," Gertrude said.

"Could you find out? There's ten bucks in it if you get lucky. I want to tell the world about the man who fought a man with bowie knives in a freshly dug grave and gunned down at least four town marshals."

"He *is* crazy, you know," Gertrude said. "They say he likes to strip his clothes off, ride like fury up and down the street on his white horse, then invite everybody into the nearest saloon for a drink."

"He's a curly wolf killer," said Gilda. "If he is around, you'd better steer clear of him."

"I can't, I've got orders from my editor."

"The marshal'd know if he's in town," Gertrude said. "I know he's been here plenty of times; no reason why he couldn't come back."

"I'd rather not bring the marshal in on this. If there's any other way of finding out without tipping my hand."

"We'll try," said both.

"For ten dollars," said Gertrude.

"And because you're cute," said Gilda.

10

Sheriff Matt Coombs changed his mind and ordered Annie Bowater—Prunella Watley—removed to Sundance and held there for trial. She protested vigorously.

Watching two deputies all but haul her bodily from her cell, Perry wondered what objection she had to Sundance; jail is jail wherever they hang up the keys. Perhaps she was angry because she'd no longer be able to keep an eye on him and contradict his every claim to innocence. She was the vindictive sort. Whatever had persuaded him to invite her into the scheme in the first place? If only she'd gotten pixilated, she might never have made it out to the sawmill to blab the truth about him. At that, he could scarcely expect the sheriff, the marshal, and the others not to recognize him as the bishop.

He'd now been behind bars nearly two full days. His conscience continued to pain him over his shabby treatment of the ministers and Father Dunphy. They had trusted him implicitly and he'd taken full advantage of it. He'd never be able to erase sight of all five walking dejectedly away, their cheeks glowing with embarrassment, leaving Rev. Miller's accusations ringing in his ears.

Thank the Lord Prunella never suspected he was carrying the $120,000. Unfortunately, although the previous day was stifling, today had to be ten degrees hotter. The marshal pointedly asked him why he didn't remove his coat.

"It's not that hot," he lied.

"Then how come you're sweating bullets? You're soaking wet. Take it off; there's a hook outside I can hang it on. Nothing'll happen to it. I'll take the responsibility. You got to sit in a cell, you should at least be comfortable."

"I'm fine, thank you."

"Take it off and lay it on the cot if you don't want me to hang it up. It's got to be ninety degrees today, a hundred in here."

"It's all right."

The marshal chuckled. "What, is the lining packed with greenbacks? Is it? Is that why you won't let go of it?"

"Of course."

"Ha, you wish."

"It looks like I'll be going on trial. Of course there isn't a judge or jury in the territory that'll find me guilty. Of what? Nevertheless, I will need a lawyer. Is there a halfway decent one in town?"

"There's Moses Aletter. He's a fox. I've seen him make a whole, entire jury cry like babies. He's not cheap, though."

"Would you contact him for me?"

"Sure."

As things were to turn out, he would be in no need of a lawyer. Before the marshal could set foot out the door, a visitor arrived. He came back to see Perry.

"Cletus," Perry said humbly, avoiding his eyes.

"Mr. Youngquist, I bring good news. Amos, Hildreth, Patrick, Ewart, and I have talked it over. We've decided not to press charges against you."

"That *is* good news. I'm very grateful, Cletus. I'm sure it was you who persuaded them."

"On the contrary, they persuaded me. There's one condition: you're to get out of Fodder City and never come back."

"Agreed."

Rev. Miller was staring at him. He had a shattered look about him, as if he'd just heard of the death of his dearest friend.

"It doesn't make sense," he said, "a man of your obvious breeding, education, intelligence, why do you stoop to such monkeyshines, fleecing people? Taking advantage of their trust in you, their confidence, lying, deceiving? Have you no conscience, man? Why do you do it? What impels you to such monstrous behavior? We accepted you in faith, made you welcome in our churches, our homes, we believed in you and you made fools of us. How do you sleep nights?"

"Not very well."

"As Christians, we can find it in our hearts to forgive you; we must, but the hurt will remain. Hopefully, in time it will go away, but never again will I be able to take the word of a stranger or give him the benefit of any doubt. I'll always be chary. You've left a mark on us all."

"I'd like to say I'm sorry, but I know it's too easy to say. Words are always the easiest part. I must make amends, somehow."

"There are acts for which no amends can be made; I'm afraid this is one such. Marshal . . ."

"Yes, Reverend?" In he came.

"Let him out."

"You're sure that's what you want."

"Not particularly, but let him out." The cell door was unlocked and swung open. "Leave Fodder City, Mr. Youngquist, and don't come back."

"Yes, Cletus."

11

Perry was still able to turn in the buggy seat, look back, and see the scene of his downfall when he came to a decision: the first town he came to, Inyankara in the shadow of Inyan Kara Mountain, he would stop and wire the entire $120,000 to Rev. Cletus O. Miller. It seemed the least he could do for them. It seemed the most Christian thing he could do for himself. T.G. wouldn't object.

With the needle of his greed he had pierced their prides, which had to be infinitely more painful than if he'd emptied their wallets. Back would go the $120,000, and maybe, just maybe, he would find some small satisfaction in it. It was at least a gesture toward restitution.

He had taken his coat off for the first time in days. It lay neatly folded in the bed of the buggy. It was a relief to get it off, both physically and mentally. On second thought, why bother wiring it back from Inyankara? Why not double back after dark, stop at the outskirts, and sneak into town and into the Congregational church and leave it in the poor box? Better yet, leave it at Cletus Miller's door, knock on the door, and run.

It wasn't all he owed them, but it wasn't chicken feed. Maybe T.G. would get lucky up in Deadwood or wherever Allison's trail led him. Maybe he'd turn the tables on the two of them and recover the proceeds and the rest of the bank's money. The boy was sharp, he'd pulled off tougher jobs in his time.

Ahead loomed Inyan Kara Mountain, but only briefly;

the road curved sharply, erasing sight of it. He felt good, the best he'd felt in two weeks. Giving the money to Rev. Miller paved the base of his stomach with satisfaction. He could never make the wrong right, but he could try to make it up to him, to all of them.

And he'd learned his lesson, never again would he trifle with a lottery con. It involved too many innocents, and too many got hurt, their faith in their fellow humans shattered, perhaps for good. He would stick to poker and the other card games, with an occasional fling at dice just to keep his hand in. He had no qualms about shearing sheep in five-card stud or draw. They wouldn't be in the game themselves if they weren't out to take him. That he was a pro, that his skills were sharper than most, didn't nettle his conscience; he'd worked his whole life to hone his edge, he earned what it gained him.

"I'm turning over a new leaf, horse, are you listening? Pericles Jubal Youngquist is abandoning the con for good. Permanently. There'll never be a sequel to this sorry experience."

He couldn't wait to place the money at Rev. Miller's door, knock, and run and hide behind a tree, if one was convenient; watch him open the door and discover the money. The amount would confuse him, but perhaps in time he'd be able to figure out how the lottery had been rigged, perhaps one of them would. Whether they did or not, having been burned, they'd never again yield to the honeyed blandishments of a con artist and jump into the trap a second time.

He had rounded the corner; the dusty road stretched reasonably straight through the mountains ahead. Out from behind an outcropping stepped two men.

"Great Caesar's ghost!" His heart sank so suddenly so low he pictured it boxed between his kneecaps.

Clay Allison and Leland.

"Will you look who's here?" boomed Allison, waggling his six-gun. "Old Mister No Name."

"What a small world," exclaimed Leland, and proceeded to dance a clumsy jig in his elation. "Wow-wheeeee!"

"Gentlemen . . ."

Allison caught the horse's rein at the cheekpiece. "How you been, old-timer? Where you been? What happened to Mr. Tilly?"

"Who knows? Ahem, would you mind not waving that hardware around so? It makes me nervous. You don't need it, I'm unarmed."

"No little peashooter in your back belt?" Leland asked.

"None. Word of honor. Can I lower my arms?"

Allison nodded. "Where 'bouts you heading?"

"Inyankara. My elder sister, Jacqueline, lives there. She was in a frightful accident: broke both legs, one arm, and fractured her pelvis, poor soul. In dreadful pain; she's expecting me. It's a pleasure seeing you both again, I'll just be on my way."

"Just hold your horse, Pop," said Allison.

"If there's something I can do for you, by all means name it." He frowned in puzzlement. "This is a surprise. I would have thought you'd be four territories away from these parts by now."

Allison shook his head, disagreeing. "Man on the run winds up getting chased by Western Union, and that little old wire's a lot faster than any horse. These hills are a lot safer than running; I know 'em every trail, every turn. We spot anybody coming after us we can lose 'em in two shakes."

"And hide out from the whole Seventh Cavalry, you bet," added Leland.

Allison leered and licked his lips. "Got any cash?"

"Are you serious? You rode away two days ago with upward of half a million dollars."

"Two days ago. We haven't turned a thin dime today, isn't that so, Lee?"

"That's so, Clay."

"How's about turning out your pockets?"

Perry flared. "You want my wallet, why don't you ask for it? I haven't got much."

"Toss it down and let's see," Allison said. Perry fought back his rising anger and complied. "Hey, there's about four hundred bucks here. What in hell you call 'not much?' "

"Gentlemen, gentlemen, what do you need with such a trifling sum? You've half a million."

"That's true," said Allison. "What do you say, Lee, should we leave him keep it?"

"All of it?"

"Half."

"I guess."

Allison extracted half and tossed back the wallet. "This is your lucky day."

"I appreciate it. Can I go now? Jacqueline's waiting. If only I get there in time . . ."

"It's only about four miles to town," Leland said.

"Go ahead," said Allison, stepping aside.

Perry rapped rump and the buggy started forward. The horse hadn't traveled more than twenty feet when Allison called out. His voice was like an icicle laid against Perry's spine.

"Hold it just a second . . ."

His heart beating furiously, Perry ground his teeth and pulled up. They came running up.

Allison grinned. "We missed your coat."

"What?"

"Your coat in the bed there," said Leland. He picked it up. "Well, I'll be jiggered! Look at this, Clay!"

"I'll be a suck egg mule, there must be fifty, sixty thousand!"

"More'n that. What you doing with all this money, Pop?"

"It's my life savings. You wouldn't take a man's life savings, would you?"

"Hell, no," said Allison. He placed all six packets in Perry's lap, then pulled his gun again. "We wouldn't take 'em, you're gonna give 'em to us." He whipped off his hat, holding it out upside-down. "Give . . ."

"Doggone!" whooped Leland. "That *is* a funny one,

that's special, that is. We're not gonna take 'em, you're gonna give 'em. I gotta remember that one; that is funny. Fun-eeee. A proper caution! Wow-wheeee!"

Perry murdered first one then the other with his eyes; he dropped the money into the hat.

Allison tossed his coat back into the buggy. "Now get outta' here."

Perry started out.

"And give our best to Jacqueline, y' hear?" bawled Leland.

"I hear, you miscreant lice, scum of the earth, thieving blaggards!"

12

Gilda and Gertrude made discreet inquiries regarding Clay Allison's whereabouts over the next two days without success. Over the two nights Horne obligingly submitted to their assaults on his body. When the morning of the third day dawned, he decided that a third night in their bed could spell disaster for him. They were insatiable; he was incapable, drained, enfeebled, useless. They refused to believe him when he described his condition; they wanted to resume playing moments after he awoke. He refused.

"We've got a deal," protested Gilda. "We look for Allison for you and you play."

"My playing days are over for the time being. If I don't quit, I'll wind up in a wheelchair. Besides, I'm wasting your time. Allison and his sidekick obviously aren't around, probably never came within fifty miles of here."

"He comes to Deadwood all the time," said Gertrude and Gilda.

"Just not this time."

"Nobody's seen him," Gilda said. "Leastwise nobody'll admit they have, not in town."

"Not out at his place," said Gertrude.

Horne sat up. "What place?"

"He's got a cabin set back off the road on the way to New Bavaria. It's behind a pine grove so you can't see it from the road."

"My God . . ."

"What's the matter?" Gilda asked. "He's not there, that's so, isn't it, Gertrude?"

"That's so."

"Where exactly is this place?"

"We told you," said Gilda and Gertrude.

"I need specific directions."

Gilda shrugged. "Don't know what good going out there would do you."

"Humor me."

"I'd say it's about four miles from the edge of town; you'll see a big pine grove. You got to go through the trees to get to the cabin."

"I've never seen it," Gertrude said, "but I hear it's nothing, little more than a shack. It's empty for weeks at a time. Nobody but a pig like Allison'd live there."

"Four miles out . . ." He jumped out of bed and began pulling his clothes on.

"You're not going out there now, are you?" asked Gertrude and Gilda.

"I've got to take a look."

"What for?" asked Gilda. "We just told you it's empty."

"I know . . . Look, don't either of you tell a soul about me going out there, okay? I don't want any pals of theirs coming to call. I just want to look around. I'll be able to see in a minute if they've been there recently. I might even find a clue to where he's gone."

"Fiddlesticks," said Gertrude. "He's not going to leave you a map on the kitchen table."

"Or a note," said Gilda. "You're just wasting your time."

"We'll see."

The roan was old, spindly-legged, worn-looking; her left eye looked a little foggy, her coat was dull, her mane a mass of tangles. At first glance she looked to Horne as if she couldn't run a hundred yards without collapsing with the heaves, but the little man with the beard too big for his face asked only fifteen dollars to rent her for the day, and he was willing to throw in a

California saddle that looked as if it had been stampeded over.

It proved to be about as comfortable as sitting on a woodpile, but the round trip to the cabin was mercifully short. Having left his .45, his .22, and his Barns boot pistol in his room at MacIvitty's in Fodder City, he bought himself a used Colt and a box of cartridges.

It was eleven o'clock by the time he left town, heading in the direction of Sturgis. The sun was approaching its zenith, the day was broiling hot, but a fleet of sullen-looking clouds was sailing in from the east. The air was clear and dry, with no hint of rain, but that could change in two hours. He could see the turnoff to the right that led east to New Bavaria.

As he'd said to Gertrude and Gilda, he'd be able to tell the minute he walked in if Allison and Leland had visited the cabin. If they had stopped off there, it would be for one purpose only: to cache the money stolen from the Miners and Merchants Bank. He espied the pine grove, cut off the road, and made his way through the trees. There sat the cabin, as ramshackle as Gertrude had implied. The right front corner looked on the verge of collapse; the roof was missing shingles and the chimney looked as if a stiff wind would topple it. The grass was high all around, and when he came closer, he could see that only one hinge supported the front door. He rode around back. The well roof had been knocked off its uprights and lay on its side in the grass. A ladder fashioned of split logs laid against poles lay against the wall under the kitchen window. The back stoop was broken, as was one of the two rear windows.

He dismounted, hobbled the horse, and went inside. He opened the back door, and a rush of foul air struck his nostrils, the stink of a dead animal. It could have been field mice, rats, anything, he thought: whatever, it was disgusting. He left the door open and, walking through the place, opened the front door wide. Allison and Leland, somebody had been there recently. The dust on the kitchen counter was disturbed and meat bones in two plates on the table had not yet rotted.

He began searching. He got a piece of kindling out of the firewood box and jammed it up the chimney, hoping to strike something solid, but there was no obstruction. He went back outside, set the ladder up, and ascended to the roof. Most of the shingles were loosened and he took pains to pick his way carefully over to the chimney to keep from slipping, falling, and possibly sliding off the roof. Reaching the chimney, he stared down it, then reached down. Nothing blocked it.

He descended the ladder and restored it to its place; he went back inside and began to search the front room. Using the pump handle as a pry, he raised one floorboard after another, taking nearly an hour to check every inch underneath. He found nothing. He did the same in the bedroom and the kitchen. He could look up and see the inside of the roof through the bare crossbeams; there looked to be no place larger than the inside of his hat to hide anything, but all four corners were shrouded in darkness, so he brought the ladder inside and checked each, lighting a match to assure himself nothing was hidden there.

In the bedroom he ripped open the straw mattress and searched every inch. He found nothing but straw. In the kitchen there were a few cans of pork and beans, a can of Standard tomatoes, four cans of Sears Roebuck Yellow Crawford peaches, and a half-filled package of Arbuckle's Ariosa Coffee. In the cabinet over the sink he found a quarter-filled bottle of Horton's rye whiskey. A single tug set his throat afire.

He searched the entire house painstakingly. When he turned up nothing, he started all over again. It was nearly five o'clock when he finally gave it up. He had not eaten since morning, so he opened a can of peaches and ate every one. He then began searching around outside, beginning with the well. The winch was ancient and the rope so rotted it threatened to snap when he hauled up the bucket. He dropped a rock and heard it splash below.

He searched a radius of a hundred yards around the house; he found nothing. He went back inside and sat in the rocker in the front room to rest, relax, and run the situation through his mind. Somebody had definitely used the place in the past few days. That somebody could have been Allison and Leland; the two plates indicated two vistors.

"Could be two squatters, T.G."

True. Both doors were unlocked, anybody happening by could walk in and take over the place, eat the food, sleep in the bed. What did it matter: The money wasn't there. Allison and Leland were probably still packing it.

T.G. sat for a long time mulling over the problem, but no solution came to him. He'd foolishly gotten his hopes up only to see them dashed. He might just as well climb on old paint, go back to town, turn in the horse, and leave Deadwood. Staying on would be pointless.

He went into the kitchen and opened a second can of peaches, but could only eat half. The syrup was too sweet; what he really needed was a steak. Thunder rumbled in the east and lightning ripped the sky, briefly brightening the interior of the cabin.

He was preparing to leave when the storm broke. He was four steps out the door, heading toward his horse, when the rain started coming down in buckets. He turned about and ran back. He stood in the doorway watching the rain batter the horse, took pity on her, ran back out, freed her from her hobbles, and led her into the kitchen. He got both pillows from the bed and wiped her down. She whinnied appreciatively.

He finished the rest of the peaches and went back out to the front room. The rain was coming down so ferociously it couldn't last more than half an hour, he decided. He sat in the chair rocking, staring at the fireplace. Staring . . . thinking . . .

Something was wrong. He couldn't put his finger on

it, but something that should be wasn't. He looked overhead. The roof leaked, not badly, just a drop sneaking through here and there and splattering on the floor. He rose from the chair and, kneeling at the fireplace, ran his hand over the hearth.

It was bone-dry.

"Oh, my God . . ."

Once again he jammed a piece of kindling up the chimney; again it touched nothing. He ran out into the kitchen, around the horse to the door. Ignoring the downpour, which showed no signs of letting up, he again placed the ladder against the back of the house and climbed to the roof. At the edge he stopped and came back down. He went back inside into the bedroom and pulled the mattress off the bedstead. He tried to break it up, but it was oak and nailed securely. Rummaging through the kitchen cabinets, he found an ax. He chopped loose one side of the bedstead and carried it outside and up the ladder. Hovering over the chimney, the rain slamming down upon him soaking him to the skin, he began pounding away with the board. He finally loosened the obstruction below. So loud was the downpour he couldn't hear it thump to rest on the hearth, but he was now able to drop the board all the way down.

In his haste to descend the ladder he nearly fell. He ran inside. Sitting on the hearth was a bulging sack.

It was nearly ten o'clock when he finished counting the contents of the sack. He had started a fire in the fireplace, hanging his coat, trousers, vest, shirt, and socks on the mantel to dry. The stench was gone and the fire made the front room cozy. He had brought the horse in to keep him company. The total amount came to $498,620. All but about four thousand dollars was in paper, the rest in gold and silver coin.

He sat in the rocker in his underwear relaxing and gloating. And thinking about Perry. He was no doubt still in jail in Fodder City. His own course was clear; he would buy himself a farm wagon and a team to haul it, attire himself as a farmer, hide the sack under a load of hay, a load of something, and drive back to Fodder City. The sack was much too big to carry on horseback; Allison and Leland had brought the money there in four bulging saddlebags. Moreover, riding it back to Fodder City, he would run the risk of being held up. Returning by stage would also be risky. A farm wagon was his best bet.

"Hang on, Perry, by this time tomorrow you'll be a free man."

He whooped aloud in triumph, picking up two handfuls of money and tossing them high. Everything had come up roses; even the storm cooperated.

Moments later it stopped raining and the stars came out.

13

No sooner had he gotten out of sight of Allison and Leland than Perry pulled up, got down, and freed the horse from the shafts. He mounted bareback and, wheeling about, started back. He espied their dust halfway up the mountainside, then their heads bobbing up and dropping below the rocks. They couldn't be just riding around aimlessly, he thought, they had to have a stopping place, even just a cave. He started up the trail after them only to stop.

"What am I doing, horse?"

He had no gun, no knife, not even a nail file. If he blundered too close, they would surely see him and blow him down a crevice. Still, while he could still see them, he couldn't let them get away. Ever since he'd met them, they'd been getting the best of him, ridiculing and insulting him, ordering him about like a slave; now they'd stolen his money, intended for the clergymen, and left him in the road helpless and fuming. How much could a man take? And from two such ignoramuses, deadbeats, thieves, murderers, useless trash!

"Giddup . . ."

The trip back had been slow, boring, and uneventful. And insidiously hot. Trundling into town, Horne headed straight for the bank, pulling up and braking in front. The lottery sign had been removed. He spotted D. Lennox Flynn coming back from lunch. He watched him start across the street, stop, gape, squint, gawk, and come running.

"You! What the devil are you doing in that getup? The marshal told us they left you at Dutton's sawmill. He and Sheriff Coombs brought back that phony bishop and his confederate, what's her name, the woman. Where did you go?"

"Is the bishop in jail?"

"He was for a while. They let him go, he left town."

"Let him go?"

"The ministers dropped the charges."

"Where's he gone?"

"Who knows? Who cares? What's with the bib overalls, that preposterous straw hat?"

"I've got something for you, Lennox." Horne climbed into the wagon bed, pulled aside the hay, and uncovered the sack. "Your money."

"Great balls of fire!" Flynn climbed up and attacked the sack, nearly ripping it in his eagerness to get at the contents. "Marvelous! Wonderful! Fabulous! Amazing! I never thought I'd see a penny again. How did you manage it? What did you do?"

His outburst and his actions began to attract a crowd. "Ladies and gentlemen," Flynn boomed, "friends, neighbors, Mr. Tillinghast here has brought back the money, every penny!"

"Wait, wait," Horne said. "I don't know about 'every penny.' Remember, quite a bit of the prize money was paid out before the holdup."

"Who cares? This is the bulk of it." He clapped him so enthusiastically, so hard on the back he nearly toppled him from the wagon. "Hero! Noble fellow! Savior of us all! Three cheers for Mr. Tillinghast!"

The crowd responded eagerly; spirited applause followed.

"How did you manage it, Edward? Don't be shy, tell us the whole story. Good Lord, you didn't shoot it out with them . . ."

"Hardly." Horne told about searching the cabin, the storm, the blocked chimney.

"Bless my soul and body, what can I say? What can

any of us? Single-handed you've saved the day. Saved Fodder City! Come inside. Make way there, folks."

Flynn carried the sack through the bank, running a gauntlet of gaping employees and customers. He brought it into his office and planted it on the desk.

"Shut that door, give us some privacy. By the way, you're entitled to a finder's fee, you know."

"I couldn't, Lennox."

"Okay. I doubt you can accept it anyway, being employed by the Banking Commission and all."

Mild shock assailed Horne; he had demurred out of simple courtesy, scarcely imagining the offer would be dropped so suddenly. He couldn't believe his hearing. No finder's fee? Not one dirty dollar?

"Lawmen can't accept rewards either, you know."

"I know. There is one small favor you can do me."

"Name it, anything."

"Out at the sawmill where the gang shot it out with the men that woman hired I met the old gentleman."

"Who?"

"The fellow they brought in, the one who posed as the bishop."

"Oh, him." Flynn paused; he crinkled his forehead questioningly. "What was he doing out there anyway?"

"He had to stop; he told me his horse had thrown a shoe. When we showed up, Allison took him hostage, too. He and I got to talking. Got to know each other pretty well during the shoot-out and after. I know you and the ministers feel he's left a bad taste in everybody's mouth . . ."

"That's putting it mildly; the sanctimonious old coot should be horse-whipped, tarred, and feathered! If he's got the brains of a fish, he'll never show his face around here again."

"He was very remorseful, Lennox—I mean, conscience-stricken. I felt sorry for him. You got your money back, the lottery committee will get its money. I'd appreciate it if you considered it a gesture on his part to make amends."

"Amends? Him? He's not returning it; you are. You're a hero, he's still dirty washing. Forget about him. All of us are trying to. The man's a parasite and a con artist. Frankly, I hope he trips and falls down somebody's dry well, the devious old reprobate."

"Don't call him that."

"Sorry, no offense. See here, you really did get thick with him out there, didn't you?"

"Does anybody have any idea where he went?"

"Nobody cares. My dear Edward, I really must do something to show my personal appreciation for this. You went to a pile of trouble for all our sakes. How's about letting me buy you lunch? What do you say? Are you hungry?"

"Not a bit," Horne lied.

"Then how about a cigar?" He began fumbling in a drawer.

"No, thanks. I don't smoke. I'll just be on my way."

"Where to?"

"My next assignment's in Newcastle. I have to stop off at MacIvitty's Lodgings and pick up my things. Incidentally, when word gets out about this, the lottery winners that didn't get paid will be coming around."

"Henrietta'll take care of them." Flynn seized his hand and pumped it vigorously. "Thanks again, Edward. I mean it from the bottom of my heart. It was mighty white and mighty brave of you to go to all this trouble. You're a genuine hero, genuine, yessir!"

"Think nothing of it," Horne said quietly.

On his way out he looked around but failed to see Henrietta Lacklund. Just as well, he thought; if she stopped him and they got to rehashing the morning of the holdup, she'd probably start questioning him about the prize money again.

On the sidewalk he stopped to light up a Jersey cheroot before heading for the marshal's office.

Perry followed Allison and Leland for nearly three hours under a broiling sun. He was dripping with perspiration and utterly exhausted; his backside ached and pain stabbed at his crotch; he was thirsty, hungry, and furious by the time they pulled up in front of a shack. He stopped, dismounted, and tied his horse to a tree limb. Crouching low, he crept through the trees to a large yellow pine thick enough to hide behind. Straining his ears, he could just barely make out what they were saying.

"I'm getting to like that old gaffer," Allison said. "He's so goddamned pitiful. He's like an old dog that can't hardly fend for itself."

"He ain't just old, he's poor now. Wow-wheee! This sure has been some week, Clay."

"It just goes to show. We been through our share o' hard times, but if you keep your nose to the grindstone, work hard, do your best, sooner or later the breaks is bound to come your way."

"You said it, partner."

Perry spat, glared, and ground his teeth.

"What we gonna do with his cash, Clay?"

"Leave it in my saddlebags. Hang on to it till we get where we're going."

"I purely love Texas. I was born in Tioga, Sherman County. My daddy growed wheat there, you betcha. He was doing right good till he got into a argument with a neighbor and shot him. They hanged Daddy. I was just a boy, only twenty-eight. Hey, what about the money we left up to Deadwood?"

"What about it?"

"Aren't we taking a chance leaving it stuck in that chimney? Neither o' the doors got locks. Anybody could come along . . ."

"So?"

"What if they was to start a fire? The smoke won't make it up the chimney; they'll know something's blocking it; they'll 'vestigate the chimney, find the sack with the half million."

Perry swallowed. Very slowly so as not to hurt his

throat. He could feel his eyes start from their sockets and his hands were trembling. "Great Caesar's ghost!"

"Nobody's gonna start no fire in August in this heat."

"Cook fire."

"No kind of fire."

"Firewood's right handy."

"Will you shut up about fire?"

Allison suddenly sounded worried, thought Perry; he obviously hadn't considered the possibility of someone starting a cook fire.

"If some dumbbell starts a fire, the place'll fill up with smoke and he'll have to put it out."

"I hope."

"He won't bother checking out the chimney; he'll figure it's just stuffed up and say to hell with it."

"I hope."

"Will you quit saying that? Nobody's gonna start no cook fire in the damn fireplace."

"We left coffee and pork and beans."

"Shut up, Lee. You're starting to rile me. I don't like being riled, so shut up!"

Perry had heard enough. Allison changed the subject; the two of them went inside.

To the devil with the $120,000, Perry thought. Suddenly there were bigger fish to fry: a half-million dollar whale! Deadwood. A cabin. If he shook a leg, he could be there in less than two hours . . .

14

Horne ate lunch and stopped off at MacIvitty's to pick up his things. He sold the team, the wagon, and his overalls, throwing in the straw hat, for twelve dollars more than he'd paid for them in Deadwood. He bought a three-year-old chestnut gelding and saddle. The man at the livery stable recalled selling Perry a horse and buggy, but had no idea where he was heading. Horne called on the marshal. He too didn't know where he was going when he let him out. He suggested he speak with Rev. Miller.

The minister welcomed him graciously.

"The news is spreading like wild fire that you got the money back, Mr. Tillinghast. I can't begin to tell you how relieved we all are. And grateful. Come in."

They sat in the parlor. Rambling roses climbed up the side window, basking in the bright sunlight. Rev. Miller offered his guest lunch, tea, a cigar, a fancy chocolate cream, a chair, all of which were politely declined save the last. The parlor was comfortable; a woman's touch was in evidence in its furnishing: the curtains were frilly and feminine, an enormous rag rug in gently clashing colors covered the floor, and matching antimacassars adorned both easy chairs. A canary twittered in its cage on a brass floor stand, and bucolic scenes in gilded frames graced three walls.

"How on earth did you find it?"

Horne repeated the explanation he'd given Flynn. "I just came from the marshal's," he said. "He told me you were the last person to talk to Mr. Youngquist and that he may have told you where he was going."

At mention of the name Rev. Miller's face darkened. "I really can't say."

"Did he say anything at all that might give a clue?"

"Not that I recall. Why do you care where he went? What is he to you?"

"My uncle."

Rev. Miller gaped. "You . . ."

"I was in on it." He explained. The minister listened, punctuating his every admission with a gentle shake of his head. "I'd appreciate it if you kept it our little secret, at least till I've left town. I can assure you I won't be coming back. You don't have to keep it secret, of course. I only ask as a favor in exchange for returning your money. It's all there except for the prize money that was paid out."

"This is a shock, Mr. Tillinghast."

"Richardson, Alistair Richardson. The lottery was a scam, I grant you, but there was never any intention of shortchanging you people, and if you think about it, none of the legitimate winners got burned."

"I'm sorry, I have to disagree. You people held out four winning tickets, including the grand prize: a hundred and twenty thousand dollars in all. If you hadn't rigged the thing, the money would have been honestly won."

"I suppose. Still, look at it this way, sixty thousand was won instead of a hundred and eighty, but the main objective, to collect money for the churches, was realized. If there never was a lottery, all of you would still be scrambling for money. Thanks to Perry you've got all you need."

Rev. Miller considered this. "Perhaps. Nevertheless, he did deliberately cheat us, the three of you in cahoots did. A crime is a crime, Mr. Richardson. There's no excusing any of you. Still, you have come forward when you didn't need to, and I am a Christian. As the Lord said in Jeremiah: 'I will forgive their iniquity and I wil remember their sin no more.'

"As for your uncle, he never mentioned where he was going, but Hildreth Lacklund did tell me he saw him leaving town in a buggy and he was heading south."

"That helps."

A knock sounded. Rev. Miller excused himself. He opened the door to Lennox Flynn; he seemed upset.

"The marshal said you'd be here, Edward. I counted the money; Henrietta and I counted it a second time together." He scowled. "I regret to say it's more than a hundred and twenty thousand short."

"I told you, most of the winners were paid off before the holdup."

"You never said 'most.' "

"I'm saying it now."

"Oh."

"Won't you come in?" asked Rev. Miller.

"No, thanks. I've got to get back." He was continuing to eye Horne questioningly.

"Most . . ."

"Most. In round numbers, a hundred and twenty thousand."

Flynn grunted, studied the tips of his boots briefly, accorded both men an indifferent wave, and walked off.

"You're quite right about the four winning tickets we held out, Reverend. Perry is probably still carrying the hundred and twenty thousand—at least it appears he left town with it. When I catch up with him, I'll see that it's returned, providing he still has it."

"That's very decent of you. It's . . . Frankly it's extraordinary. If you don't mind my asking, what's behind this change of heart?"

"I don't know. I guess I just want to wipe the slate clean. It doesn't make sense to return most of the money and not all. Not to me. It won't to Perry, either, after I talk to him. It's a little hard to explain, but sometimes the two of us do things that end up sticking in our craws. This is one. I didn't feel comfortable about it from the start. I don't know." He got up from his chair. "I guess I'll be going."

Again Rev. Miller offered him a candy. He accepted.

"Good luck, Mr. Richardson, and Godspeed. And don't worry, I can keep a secret." He grinned. "We all wondered how you rigged the thing; we should have known you concocted fictitious winners."

"It's always the safest way in any lottery; it's foolproof."

They shook hands.

Perry stood at the bar in the Green Front Sporting House talking to the bartender and sipping bourbon.

"I'm on roving assignment for my publisher. Perhaps you've heard of Beadle and Adams?"

The bartender's eyes glowed. "You're with Beadle and Adams?"

"Head of the plot department. My staff and I supply the plots for the writers. I'm look for Calamity Jane Cannary. I hear she's around. We're planning a whole new series based on her experiences."

"I haven't seen Jane in Deadwood in three years. Beadle and Adams . . . I read your books all the time. I got one right here, matter of fact." He fumbled under the bar and held up *Kansas King or the Red Right Hand* by Buffalo Bill. "You know Buffalo Bill personally?"

Perry held up two fingers tightly aligned. "Like my brother. Have you read *The Dread Shot Four, or My Pards of the Plains* by Bill?" The bartender shook his head. "You should, it's a corker. What's your name?"

"Jack Finley."

"Let me send you a copy, Jack. I'll get Bill to autograph it."

"Wow!"

"Say, if Jane's not around, is anybody else? Bill Hickock, Wyatt Earp?"

The bartender squinched up his face and pondered. "Clay Allison. I didn't actually see him, but word around town is he was here. Another fellow was asking after him."

"Is that so? Young fellow, mustache, dark eyes, complexion?" He described Horne further.

"That's him," said a voice behind Perry. He turned. Gertrude smiled. "Mr. Richardson. He's a reporter with the Associated Press in New York City."

"Where is he now?" Perry asked. "I'd like to meet him. We might be able to help each other."

"He's long gone."

"Did he say where?"

"Nope."

Gilda had come up beside Gertrude. They were dressed identically in shamrock green with single white ostrich feathers in their high-piled hair and matching gold hearts suspended from slender chains.

"He went out to Allison's cabin to look around," Gertrude said.

"That's the last we saw of him," said Gilda and Gertrude.

"Cabin?"

"Out on the road to New Bavaria," said Gilda. She gave him directions.

"Thank you kindly," Perry said excitedly. "Thank you very much. Very much. I appreciate it. I do. Thank you!"

And he was gone.

He pulled the buggy into the pines, tied the horse to a limb, and walked through to sight of the cabin. So T.G. had been there. Unquestionably looking for the stolen money. Had he found it? Was it even there? If it was, had he failed to find it? It wouldn't do any harm to check.

The place was a rathole, but there was ample evidence that it had recently been occupied. The rotting bones on the plates in the kitchen, the two empty Sears Roebuck Yellow Crawford peach cans. The bed was wrecked; one of the stead side boards was missing. Somebody had lit a fire in the fireplace recently. Perry cleaned off the hearth, lay a pillow on it, and getting down on his back, looked up the chimney. He could see the sky clearly. No money there.

He went out back and checked the well. There was water, he wound up a bucketful. He went back inside, then into the front room. He examined the rafters overhead. As he craned his neck and squinted into a darkened corner through the soft melodious murmur of the breeze he heard hoofbeats. He glanced out the window.

"Great Caesar's ghost!"

Perry ran out the kitchen door, but the empty terrain as far as he could see offered no cover. A rider came galloping around each side of the house. They pulled up in front of him.

"Will you look who's here, Lee? Old folks!"

"In the flesh, Clay. What you doing here, Pop?"

"Looking for a real-estate investment. This property looks to be exactly what I want. I'll have to tear down the cabin, of course, but the land is ideal for sheep ranching. Plenty of grass, water. I predict this whole area along the Wyoming border will one day be opened up to sheep."

"Shut up. Go back into the house, Lee. Take a look."

Leland dismounted and ran inside. And came back out immediately. "It's gone!"

Allison nodded slowly; an evil expression hardened his face. "What have you done with it, old man?"

"With what?"

Allison dismounted. "Don't play games with me. My sense o' humor just run outta the bottle. For the last time, where's the money?"

"Money?"

Allison jerked out a pistol, swung it, and cracked Perry in the right cheek.

"Owww!" He staggered back, his fingers going to his face. "You've broken it."

"I'll break the other, I'll break your head into little pieces if you don't start talking."

"I haven't seen any money. Word of honor, not a penny. I admit I came here to look for it . . ."

Leland pulled his gun, aimed it squarely at Perry's face, and cocked it.

"I'm telling you the truth! How could I possibly take it? What have I done with it?"

"Buried it," Allison said flatly.

"That's nonsense."

"I'm gonna blow your head off, Pop," Leland said.

"No you don't," Allison said. He stuck out his hand and lowered the gun. "That won't get us beans. Old man, for the last time, are you gonna tell us or do I have to beat it outta you?"

"I'm telling you the truth, damn you! My cheek is broken . . . You scum, you filthy mongrel!"

Allison took two strides toward him. Perry started back. Allison grabbed his shirtfront and held him.

"You asked for it."

15

They looked like father and son. Both wore imported Irish-linen suits, full-shape crusher hats, and mustaches, the older one's full and luxurious, the younger's somewhat sparse and struggling to catch up. They shared the upholstered seat of a shiny new Columbus phaeton buggy with a leather quarter top, fancy nickel-plated lanterns, and wide fenders. Despite their similarity in appearance, they were not father and son. The older man was a crackerjack sales representative with the Logan & Detwiler Organ Company of Cincinnati, the younger one an apprentice salesman.

"Number sixty-one is far and away our biggest seller. Eleven stops, diaposa, principia, dulciana, melodia, the whole range up to and including vox humana. An amazing instrument, George. With the dulciana and cremona stops only, you get a tone so soft, yet so clear and distinct, so sweet, it suggests ethereal voices. It's as close to heavenly music as you can get on this earth."

"That's a good line. I like that, Larry."

"That's what I always say to the prospect. Finest grade of reeds, all hundred and twenty-two, finest felt, leather, every part. Now, if it's looks that strike their fancy, you talk about the . . ."

"Cut-glass mirror."

"Correction, the rectangular French plate mirror. Any time you can get a foreign mention in there, something European, do so. It smacks of old and reliable, Old World dignity. What else for looks?"

"Bevel-face celluloid stop knobs."

"Good."

"Nickel-plated pedal frames."

"Good."

"Extension lamp shelf and handles."

"And . . ."

"The Brussels carpet thrown in."

"Not 'thrown in,' George, additional feature offered at no additional charge."

"Additional feature offered at no additional charge."

"Good, and don't forget to mention that the sixty-one has no cheap pressed designs. All designs are artistically cut into the wood by our factory artisans. Your choice in solid antique quartered oak or black walnut."

"Guaranteed not to crack or warp."

"Right, and all that for an organ worth a mere hundred and twenty-five dollars plus shipping. Which we sell, and you always pause here, we sell for a paltry seventy-eight dollars. A saving of forty-seven dollars. Of course, what the customers don't know—and they'll never find out from us—is that Sears Roebuck sells the same number for forty-four dollars."

"How do they do it, Larry?"

"Search me. They undercut everybody, whatever the item, whatever the price. Where do you think I got this suit? They . . . What's that?"

Up ahead and to the right a large black object lay in the rain ditch. Larry snapped the reins. The phaeton lurched forward. In the ditch lay a man, huddled and motionless. Larry pulled up. Both got down.

"Is he dead?" George asked in a tremulous voice.

"He sure looks it." Larry knelt and examined him. "He's still breathing, barely. Get the canteen out of the toolbox."

Perry moaned when they turned him over, and Larry raised his head. He tried to give him water, but most of it spilled.

"He's been beaten," George said. "Look at the bruises, look at his cheeks."

Again Perry moaned. "Take it easy, fella," said Larry.

"T.G. . . . Fodder City . . . Cletus Miller . . . Reverend Cle . . . Richardson . . ."

George gaped. "What's he saying?"

"Sssssh. He's fainted. Get the lap robe, hurry. He's in shock."

Horne had ample time to think on his way to Inyankara. Think, theorize, reach conclusions. Why, he wondered, had Perry headed south after his release from jail? Knowing as he did that he was heading east after Clay Allison and Leland. Knew or could reasonably assume he'd wind up in or near Deadwood? Weighing all the factors, T.G. concluded that Perry had headed south because Inyankara was the nearest town to Fodder City, and rather than linger in Fodder City to send a telegram to Deadwood inquiring as to his whereabouts, he'd elected to move on to where, unlike Fodder City, nobody would recognize him. He could have headed west to Sundance; it was closer, but Sheriff Coombs was there and Perry'd probably rejected it because he didn't want to risk another meeting with him.

Inyankara was tiny, with fewer than two hundred permanent residents, but like Fodder City, it was a magnet to the silver miners working the surrounding hills.

Horne made inquiries for two hours. No one of Perry's description had arrived in town or, from what he could gather, even passed through. With his mane of snow-white hair and distinguished profile, not to mention his deep, mellifluous voice, Perry hardly melted into the crowd; quite the contrary, anyone who so much as passed him on the sidewalk would not fail to remember him. But in Inyankara no one had.

Horne ended his tour of inquiry at the Western Union office. The clerk at the counter had a clear view of Main Street and the traffic. Like everyone else, he had no recollection of an elderly man fitting Perry's description. The conclusion was inevitable: he'd never reached town. Had he changed his mind and his direction? Had something happened to him? Had he been held up? He was carrying the $120,000. A decidedly mixed bag of characters roamed the area. Had he turned east toward Welcome? Had he turned around and headed for Deadwood? That seemed the best possibility.

T.G. mounted and started back the way he came. He would stop in Fodder City long enough to get a wire off to Deadwood to Gertrude and Gilda, care of the Green Front Sporting House. He would ask them to wire him collect if they'd seen Perry; better, tell them to tell him to contact him immediately.

He turned a corner and Inyankara vanished from sight behind him. He could hear hoofbeats. The road ahead meandered, so he was almost up to the next curve before a lone rider appeared. Rev. Cletus Miller.

"Mr. Richardson. Praise be, I've found you!"

"Reverend . . ."

He waved a telegram. "I got this not twenty minutes ago." He handed it to Horne. It had been sent from Deadwood by someone named L. Sturdivant of the Logan & Detwiler Organ Company.

> REVEREND MILLER STOP ELDERLY MAN BRUTALLY BEATEN FOUND IN DITCH ON NEW BAVARIA ROAD STOP BARELY ABLE TO SPEAK STOP MENTIONED YOUR NAME FODDER CITY NAME RICHARDSON INITIALS T G STOP IDENTITY IN WALLET P YOUNGQUIST STOP BROUGHT SAME TO DOCTOR OLIVER BLUE DEADWOOD STOP HAS REGAINED CONSCIOUSNESS ONLY ONCE SINCE TO REPEAT ABOVE STOP CONDITION VERY GRAVE STOP BLUE DOES NOT EXPECT HIM TO LIVE THROUGH NIGHT

"Perry," Horne rasped. "Who is this Sturdivant?"

"He sold us an organ last year. He's the field representative for the company. Knows just about every clergyman for a hundred miles around."

"I appreciate this, Cletus, going to all this trouble."

"What else would anyone do but go looking for you?"

"I'll have to get over there as fast as I can. God help me, I hope I'm in time."

"Who would do such a terrible thing to a helpless old man? Oh . . ."

"Allison, right. Thanks again." T.G. started off.

"Godspeed. My prayers go with you. Keep in touch."

He picked up his hand and the spots slid off the cards, fell to the table, and vanished, leaving him with five white blanks. He checked the table: no spots; under the table: none. "It's to you," growled the balding gorilla seated across from him. He started to respond, but the man pulled out a gun and emptied it into his chest. He felt nothing, then was lifted out of his chair, bumping his head on the ceiling, falling back down sprawling, and discovering bars all around him. The floor tilted precariously, sending him sliding into the bars, then he began bouncing around, striking the ceiling, the floor, the bars. He was in a giant chuck-a-luck cage; the instant he identified it, it vanished in a puff of smoke. An ear-splitting explosion followed, sending him flying across a valley lined with green beize. He landed on a faro spread, sliding across it into a dealing box. It flew apart the instant he entered, propelling him into a storm of falling cards the size of billiard tables, and chips as big as roulette wheels. One directly beneath him grew even bigger. Bigger yet and magically changing into a roulette wheel. His body tightly scrunched, he became the ivory ball, bouncing and clacking as the wheel spun. Faster and faster it whirled, spinning him out of it, flying through the air again, landing with a thump in a huge barrel. A gigantic hand reached down, seized him by the collar, lifted him up bodily, but somehow by some insidious black magic, between the moment he was seized and the moment he cleared the rim of the barrel, his body vanished and he became a ticket about the size of a coffin. A lottery ticket . . .

Dr. Oliver Blue stared down at him pityingly. He gently patted the livid bruises on his forehead and cheeks with a damp cloth. Perry slept on, his expression rigidly fixed in agony, his breathing ominously shallow and rapid.

"What you see isn't the half of it," said the doctor. "Inside, he's a mess, a disaster. He's been here seven hours and the only thing I've been able to do is stop the internal bleeding, and I didn't; it just stopped of its own accord."

"Will he make it?"

Dr. Blue took off his specs, slipped them into his breast pocket, and pursing his lips tightly, fought back a yawn. Horne judged him to be about fifty; he looked sixty and at the moment was acting even older. Fighting losing battles had that effect on medical men, he knew; out of pride they strove to win every one, even the toughest, and few looked to be tougher than this.

"I can't lie to you. I doubt he will; I know there's nothing more I can do for him. There are more than two hundred bones in the human body. His at the moment is like a suitcase full of dice. You could grab him by the toes and curl him up like a jelly roll. What isn't busted is cracked, what isn't cracked is bruised; he's got more pain per square inch than any man I've ever seen. I'm amazed he's still alive. That he's as old as he is makes it downright miraculous. Still, I can't believe he'll make it. Whoever did this ought to be boiled alive. Whoever did it is an animal."

"Clay Allison."

"Allison? Is he around Deadwood again?"

"He and one of his men did this. I'd give ten years off my life to know where they are now."

So strong was the smell of ammonia that it caused Horne to tear and made him slightly nauseous. He sat by the open window gulping fresh air. The odor didn't seem to bother the doctor. He appeared to know his business, Horne decided, after arriving and talking to him briefly. He also seemed to have done everything he could for Perry: made him as comfortable as one could be with so much pain, given him a shot of morphine to dull the pain, mopped the sweat from his face with a damp cloth. If only he could be more optimistic . . .

"If he makes it through the night, that'd be a good sign, wouldn't it?"

"Would it? Or would it be just prolonging the agony? Don't misunderstand, Mr. Richardson, I'm not trying to be flip, nor am I playing dumb; it's just that I can't do anything to help and it sticks in my craw. Frankly, in his condition I'm afraid to touch him. It really is enormously frustrating. I'm a doctor, I'm supposed to help people. A four-year-old child could pat him on the face."

"If you want to take a break, if there's something you have to do, I'll take over."

"I would like to get something to eat. Can I bring you something back?"

"No, thanks. I'm not hungry."

"You're his nephew?"

"And friend. My best friend. I wish to God I knew where Allison's gotten to."

"Hungry for vengeance, eh? That won't do him any good."

"It'll do wonders for me."

Blue shrugged. "There's water in that tin pitcher on the corner table. Wet his lips every so often. I'll be back in a bit." He stood staring at Perry. "What a mess. I've seen miners caught in cave-ins in better shape. Thank goodness he's out; if he comes to he'll never be able to stand the pain."

He put his hat on and left. Horne moistened Perry's lips, then resumed patting his face with the cloth. He was lifting it from his chin when Perry moved his head slightly and his lips.

"Allison . . ."

"I'm here, Perry."

"T.G."

Horne's heart jumped; he recognized him! His eyes had opened just a slit.

"Easy, Perry."

"Hurts like . . . blazes . . ."

"Don't talk. Save it till later."

"What later? I'm . . . dying . . . cashing in . . ."

"The hell you are. You're getting better by the hour. You'll be on your feet in no time. Don't talk, try to sleep."

"T.G., he . . . Allison . . . thought I stole . . . the money . . . from shack. Never . . . saw . . . a dime . . ."

"Where are they heading?"

"Don't . . . know . . ."

"What did they say? Anything? Maybe a direction?"

"Ti . . . oga."

"Tioga! Where, what state?"

Perry's head fell to one side, his eyes slowly sealed. For a second Horne thought he had died.

"Perry!"

He could neither see nor hear if he was still breathing. He lay one ear gently against his heart. It was beating; he was breathing.

"Tioga where?"

Dr. Blue came in. He brought him back a steak sandwich. "I figured you were too polite to ask." Horne offered him a dollar; Blue waved it away.

"I appreciate it, Doctor."

"Don't be in a hurry, wait'll you taste it. If you can eat a board, you shouldn't have any trouble with one of Ike Dawson's steaks. How's our friend doing?"

"He woke up for a few seconds. I asked him if he had any idea where they were heading."

"You shouldn't have asked him anything! What are you, blind? Can't you see he's in agony? Speaking is an effort. Makes it even more painful. What's the matter with you, don't you care?"

"I'm sorry."

"Just can't wait to go chasing after that animal, right?"

"Is there a Tioga around here?"

"Never heard of one. What makes you think they'd hang around after pulling this stunt?"

"They stole a lot of money; they hid it in Allison's

cabin; I found and returned it to Fodder City; Perry here didn't know; he came looking for it; they showed up, and when they couldn't find it . . . You get the picture. Tioga . . ."

"Go across the street to the marshal's office. Maybe he knows. He's got maps. First eat your sandwich before it gets cold. Eat it if you can bite it, that is."

Marshal O. Z. Lanigan had maps; he appeared to have a passion for collecting them. Rolled up individually, they nearly filled a good-sized closet. He was eager to cooperate with any effort that might rid the world of Clay Allison and anyone associated with him.

"You got my permission to blow the bastahd's head off if you catch up with him. Everytime he comes to Deadwood he brings trouble. He's not a man, he's a disease. I, for one, wish to hell he never left Tennessee."

Marshal Lanigan was short and round with a belly that poked his belt buckle well out in front of him. As he sat in his chair, his pistol had somehow worked its way around front and the barrel now rested in his crotch. If, thought Horne, his gun accidentally went off, he'd regret it mightily the rest of his days, but he seemed to take no notice of the shift in positions.

"Tioga . . . don't sound familiar."

For the next four hours they spread one map after another on the floor, held them in place with their knees, and painstakingly went over every inch, looking for Tioga. There was none in Dakota Territory, in Wyoming, Colorado, Montana, Idaho, or Utah. There was none in California. None in Iowa, Nebraska, or Kansas. None in Wisconsin, Illinois, Missouri, Tennessee, or Kentucky.

"Here she is," boomed Lanigan. "Sherman County, Texas. Look, right down there almost on the border of McKinney County. Tioga!"

"That's one. Keep looking."

"What for? You want Tioga, I found you Tioga."

"There could be more than one."

There was. Further searching turned up Tiogas in Louisiana and New York State.

"They can't have gone to New York," Horne said. "It's got to be either Texas or Louisiana."

"What'll you do, flip a coin?"

"I got a hunch it's Texas."

"That's a mighty long ride on a bald hunch."

"So is Louisiana."

"There could be others. We still haven't looked at Oregon, Washington, Mississippi, New Mexico . . ."

Horne got up. Pain shot up both legs to his hips; his knees throbbed, he'd been kneeling for so long. "I'm going back to Dr. Blue's and see how Perry's doing."

"In the meantime I'll check around town. Maybe somebody can connect Tioga with Allison and What's-his-name . . ."

"Leland, I don't know his last name. Much obliged, Marshal."

To Horne's surprise and elation, not to mention relief, Perry had regained consciousness. A hint of color had returned to his cheeks, but his face still looked deeply drawn with pain. He complained of difficulty in breathing; not surprising for one with fourteen broken ribs.

"T.G. . . . ooooooo."

"Don't talk," Blue said irritably. "If you must, whisper. And make it short. I'm going to have to put you under again."

"I've . . . been under. . . two full days."

"It's time I started setting a few bones. If I don't, you'll come out of this looking like a pile of kindling."

Horne leaned over him. "Perry, where's Tioga?"

"Texas. Leland's . . . ahhhhh . . . home base. They're . . . heading . . . Texas. You're . . . not . . . after them . . ."

"It's crossed my mind."

"Don't . . . be an . . . idiot. They'll . . . see . . . coming . . . kill you . . . before you . . . get near.

Ahhhh . . . not going!" He winced and grimaced in pain. "Not!"

"Will you calm down?" flared Blue. "Getting all worked up is all you need. And will you get out of here!"

Horne nodded. "You're going to be okay, Perry. I've seen him like this before, Doctor. It's a sure sign he's recovering."

"Out!"

"I'm going, I'm going. Get well, Perry, meet me in Kansas City in six weeks."

"Idiot! Ooooooo . . ."

"See you."

T.G. stood outside and lit his last Jersey cheroot. Tioga, Texas. It would be a long trek, upward of nine hundred miles. Allison and Leland would ride it; the mere thought of sitting a horse that long distance sent a tremor up his spine. He'd go by rail, thank you, only that took money. He counted his: less than thirty dollars. He turned to face the door to the infirmary.

Perry must have some money left. Whatever he had, he'd never give it to him, not to go chasing after their nibs. He could use at least a couple hundred. He knew just where to get it.

16

Perry was seventy-two and he had never paid much attention to his health. He shunned fresh air in favor of rooms filled with cigar smoke; he drank everything brewed, distilled, or fermented that gave promise of setting the inner man aglow. He religiously avoided fresh fruit and vegetables when anything fried or salted, overcooked or underripe was available. Exercise was anathema to him and a good night's comfortable sleep a rarity. Timely and proper treatment for whatever ailed him was invariably postponed or avoided altogether. For all his mistreatment and neglect of his body, he was surprisingly rugged. As tough as gristle and, for the most part, as healthy as any man half his age. Added to this blessing was a stubborn streak that made any jackass Horne had ever known seem overly cooperative in comparison. When Perry died, he would go agreeably. Six bullets from Clay Allison's gun would never kill him, a brutal beating at his or any other's hands would never nudge him off this mortal coil for the simple reason that he would refuse to give his tormentor the satisfaction of conquering him.

So it was in this case. In the time Horne spent in the marshal's office Perry had bounced back with astonishing rapidity. He was still in a bad way, he wouldn't even be hobbling in at least a month, but his mind had cleared, his feistiness had returned, and he unquestionably looked to be on the mend.

Maybe, thought Horne, he should go back and ask him for travel money.

No.

Upon leaving Dr. Blue's infirmary, T.G. went straight to the Green Front Sporting House. No poker game was going on, so he repaired to Nutthall and Mann's No. 10 Saloon. Four locals were bumping heads at draw. He kibitzed for a while. One of the players, who looked surprisingly like Marshal Lanigan, built like him, sprouting the identical generous nose and similarly colored hair, got to talking to him between hands.

"You ever see cards like this in all your born days? Every hand's worse than the one before."

"There certainly are days like that," Horne responded amiably.

"I can't pull a court card to save my life."

"Stop bitching, Obadiah," said the man seated opposite him. He was wearing a three-day beard, a patch over one eye, and a skin of trail dust that hinted he'd ridden all the way up from Mexico. "I'm out twice as much as you are. Getting no cards at all ain't half as bad as getting enough to keep you in the hand."

The other two players were a large, round-shouldered youth, missing half his teeth and displaying an unexplained black eye, and a surly ranch hand wearing hair chaps and a calico shirt with a torn pocket and sucking on an ivory toothpick. The marshal's look-alike, Obadiah, invited Horne to sit in. Horne's eyes touched those of the other three players in quest of agreement. No one disagreed. He took a chair with his back to the wall between Obadiah and Black Eye. Trail Dust smiled a greeting; Surly narrowed his eyes.

"This is a friendly game, brother, no rabbit-hunting, sandbagging, angling, mouth-betting, roodling, cross-roading, hand-mucking, bottom-dealing, crimping, or stacking. I'm wearing a gun and I know how to pull the trigger."

"It sounds like a friendly game," Horne said.

"Don't mind him," said Obadiah. "He swallowed a spider in his beer."

"And no professionals," Surly added.

"I haven't seen any yet," Horne said.

The others laughed. He bought twenty dollars' worth of chips. He anteed a dollar for draw and Surly dealt him a runt, a useless spread with not even a small pair. He tossed it in. Nineteen dollars. Obadiah won the pot with three fives. He needed the lift; it did wonders for his morale.

"Seven-toed Pete," said Black Eye.

Luck smiled. Horne was dealt an ace-four in the hole and another ace first card up.

"Ace bets," said Black Eye.

"Two dollars."

Everyone stayed. Horne's fourth card was the four of clubs. Two pair.

"Pair of sixes bet," said Black Eye, glancing at Surly.

"Two dollars," Surly said.

Horne saw him. Obadiah dropped out, leaving four players. Horne's fifth card was a queen. Surly's, a third six. He beamed triumphantly.

"Five bucks!"

"Wait, wait," cautioned Black Eye, and dealt the last card to himself. "I drop."

Horne and Trail Dust saw Surly. He reacted with visible resentment, either hoping they would drop or that one or the other would raise him.

"I got the winning hand right here," he gloated.

Sixes full? wondered Horne. The six of diamonds had shown itself among Black Eye's discards. He should have thrown in facedown, but did it; not only was it a friendly game, it was an amateur's game, Horne reflected gratefully. He got another ace on the sixth card. Aces full. Surly roared when his card landed. If he hadn't filled before he just did, mused Horne. Filled only, he certainly hadn't pulled the case six.

Surly bet ten dollars. Horne bought more chips, but had only enough money left to see him. Anger churned his stomach. How he'd love to raise him! They were the only two players left. Horne drew a deuce on his last card, dealt facedown. Whatever Surly drew had no effect on his hand either. Once again he bet ten dollars, then quickly changed his mind, making it twenty.

Horne drew twenty dollars from the pot.

"Light," he murmured.

Surly glared. "You got any money left? You sure you can cover that?"

"I'd dearly love to bump you ten more, but this being a friendly game, I'll not retract my see."

"Hey, go right ahead and bump, wise guy, and see what I bump you back."

"I'm mortally afraid of your full house."

"You gotta right to be." He lay down his hand. "Sixes full of treys. I win!" Out shot two hands the size of ball gloves. Horne laid his atop them. Surly's eyes widened, dark furrows spread across his brow.

"Aces full," said Horne.

Surly dropped out three hands later. From when he lost with his sixes full to when he folded for good, his hand must have wandered to his Colt twenty times. Every time it did Horne stiffened. He was not wearing either his .45s or his .22 Sharps. Only his Barns .50 in its boot holster, and his dagger-mounted knuckle-duster in his vest pocket protected him. Why the other players had even permitted Surly to sit down wearing a gun mystified him. Whatever their reasons, he had done so, and Horne breathed considerably easier when he quit the game without once drawing his gun.

He won four of the six hands following Surly's departure and quit himself better than $250 ahead. He left Nutthall and Mann's counting his money. Surly was waiting outside.

"Big winner, huh?" he snarled.

"Two forty, forty-five, fifty-five and thirty . . . Oh, hello again."

"You're a professional. I can smell the sissy stink o' one a mile away, and you're one."

"Sorry to disappoint you, you must have me confused with someone else."

"You cheated me."

"How could I? I wasn't dealing."

"You was holding out cards." His hand was moving slowly toward his gun.

"What exactly do you want, fellow?"

"My money, what do you think?"

"And if I don't give it to you, you'll shoot me right here in broad daylight with twenty witnesses looking on."

"Gimme my twenty-eight bucks!"

"Hi-yah, boys," Marshal Lanigan said pleasantly. Up he came. Obadiah, Black Eye, and Trail Dust came out of the saloon.

"This gentleman seems to think I cheated him," Horne said mildly. "Did I?" he asked the others.

"Out an' out," Surly boomed.

"Did like hell," said Obadiah. The others agreed and shook their heads. Surly hesitated, growled, glared, and stalked off. Horne followed him with his eyes.

"Best steer clear of Arleigh," said the marshal. "Man's got the disposition of a snake-bit wolf."

"Well put," said Horne, and waving to all, he walked off.

An hour later he was on a Chicago & Northwestern train, heading south, having disposed of his horse and saddle and purchased a left-hand holster for his second .45. He sat back and watched the Strawberry Range approaching and wondered.

Tioga, Texas, Leland's home base, according to Perry, but was that where the two of them were heading? Was it even a scheduled stop on the way? Texas was so big, there were so many places to hole up. Would he ever catch up with them?

He would; he wouldn't stop searching until he did if it took him a year. By that time the $120,000 would have melted away, to be sure, but that wasn't the primary lure, much as he wanted to recover it. Allison was the prize. For Perry. Catch him, cut off his head, stuff it, mount it on a board, and present it to Perry.

He in turn could give it to D. Lennox Flynn. He could hang it on the wall over the vault door.

"T.G., you're a card."

He chuckled to himself. He felt eyes on him. He cleared his throat in embarrassment and looked around. Looked across the aisle, looked up it and down. In the last seat on the other side a newspaper was raised, concealing the reader. As Horne noticed it it lowered.

Surly Arleigh leered.

"Oh, my God," murmured Horne.

17

Perry finished his chicken broth, draining the dregs loudly through a glass straw. He still hurt, his entire body from pate to soles felt like one big ache.

"Even my hair hurts," he said to Dr. Blue. "Is that possible?"

"You're amazing."

"I know, you keep telling me. What you fail to consider is that my whole life I've taken superb care of myself. I'm a model of physical fitness; fresh air, a rigid diet, near total abstinence . . ."

"Poppycock! If I had a microscope and examined your blood, I'd bet my horse and buggy it'd show two-thirds alcohol."

"You'd lose. My nephew didn't drop by while I was asleep, did he?"

"Wouldn't I have told you if he did? It's quarter to seven; by now he's left town."

"Hotheaded pup! Blithering idiot! He'll get his head blown off. He's no match for that maniac, no match for a twelve-year-old. He doesn't know how to fight, wrestle, defend himself in any way; he can't hit the side of a barn with a gun; he can't even run from trouble he's so glue-footed. He's a total loss. I'll never see him again."

"He's young, he's strong—"

"He's got two left feet and the reflexes of a cow. I'm going to have to get after him."

"That's a laugh. You haven't strength enough to get to the door."

"Seriously, he's never been up against a cold-blooded killer like Allison. He won't know how to handle him."

"Maybe he won't catch up with them."

"Of course he will. Anybody can. Allison trails a reputation like the red flag at the end of a long wagon load. Why do you suppose he cleared out of this neck of the woods? It wouldn't surprise me if he ended up in Mexico. T.G., you idiot, give it up. You hear me, son, he'll blow you apart."

"Want some more chicken broth?"

"No, thanks. You know something? The only thing the boy has going for him is wits. That he has, God bless him, wits."

It was dark by the time the train pulled into Rapid City. The conductor appeared at the head of the car and announced a ten-minute stopover. Five passengers sprang from their seats and retrieved their belongings lodged in the overhead racks.

The town nestled at the foot of the Black Hills on the Rapid River. It was surrounded by sprawling cattle ranches and farms. Horne studied the layout of the station platform. It looked to have been recently refurbished; the station itself was brick and the platform was covered by a roof supported by stanchions. A sign over the station door announced that food and beverages were available inside. Another sign warned that THE BELL RINGS 2 MINUTES BEFORE THE TRAIN STARTS. A wide swath of pale-yellow light fell through the open doors onto the platform. From where he was sitting Horne could not see inside. At least twenty passengers got off the train; half that number were preparing to board. He threw a look back down the aisle. Arleigh was still sitting engrossed in his newspaper. Horne was impressed. Recalling their brief association earlier, he never would have imagined that the man could read. Again he looked at the station entrance, at the moment clogged with two-way traffic. He studied the platform left and right of the building. No lights showed, indicating there were no windows at the sides.

He could get off by way of the door two seats ahead of him; instead, he elected to walk all the way back down the aisle to the end door alongside which Arleigh was sitting by himself. A man and woman preceded Horne. He was about to pass through the door into the vestibule when Arleigh lowered his paper and growled.

"Twenty-eight bucks. I'm going to get it if I have to kill you."

"You're ugly."

It was not a response he expected. He glowered fiercely in lieu of a comeback. Horne snickered, passed through the door, and descended the steps. Pausing on the platform, he looked both ways. He started to his right. Inside the station white-garbed waiters were dispensing coffee, drawing it from tall brass urns topped by eagles and proclaiming the Great American Tea Company's celebrated Sultana coffee. Travelers paid when they ordered; some caterers, according to Perry, bribed conductors to cut the stop short so that uneaten, but paid-for, food could be saved.

The street entrance to the station loomed on the far side of the square counter. He did not enter; instead, he continued walking to his right to the darkened corner of the building. He rounded it and took up his position behind the roof stanchion standing about six feet from the wall. He got out his right-hand Colt, gripping it by the barrel. He waited. Seconds ticked soundlessly by. Sweat cooled his upper lip, his heart thudded in his chest. He raised the gun overhead. He could hear the activity on the platform: voices, the wheezing of the engine at a standstill, a baggage cart trundling along, a woman's shrill laughter. He waited. Presently Arleigh appeared, reaching the corner, hesitating, casting about, then turning down the side of the building. Horne stiffened behind his concealment. Arleigh had drawn his gun. Horne let him pass, stepped from behind the stanchion, and hammered him once. Arleigh moaned softly and dissolved in a heap.

Horne restored his gun to its holster and Arleigh's to his and picked him up. He was out cold. He was also surprisingly heavy. Supporting him as best he could with his left hand under his left armpit, his right arm across his chest, Horne dragged him upright down the darkened side of the building, around the corner, and in through the street entrance. Coffee drinkers and a couple of countermen stared quizzically as he moved inside with his lifeless burden. By now his left arm ached so from the deadweight that it threatened to part from his shoulder.

"I always say, if a man can't hold his liquor he shouldn't drink."

"Amen to that, brother," said a short man pleasantly and cooperatively.

Leaning Arleigh against the counter and catching his breath, Horne looked around. To the right stood the ticket window. Tacked on either side of it were wanted posters. Even at a distance he was able to recognize Clay Allison. So the posters were out, were they? How far out? All the way down to Texas? He hoped not, hoped he could settle his score before the law settled its own. In the far corner to the right the necessary door beckoned. Getting hold of his burden, he started for it, talking to Arleigh, gently chiding him for his overindulging, and repeating his observation on drinking to the curious who eyed them, prompting nods, sounds of disapproval, and the shaking of heads. He got to the door and inside. A man had just finished and was coming out.

" 'Smatter with your freind?" he asked.

"Snoot full."

"Oh, my. Duck his face in the water bowl."

"I'm going to."

The man chuckled and left. Horne lay Arleigh on the floor and locked the door. Then he slipped Arleigh's belt from its loops, bound his ankles, and dragging him over to the cubicle door, opened it, lifted his legs high, and slipped the belt over the inside hook. Arleigh's only reaction to his efforts was a prolonged groan.

Horne was climbing out the window facing the street when the bell announcing the imminent departure of the train sounded. He began counting; thirty seconds later he was back in his seat. At 120 the whistle let loose two long blasts, the signal to proceed. Steam whooshed loudly, briefly obscuring view of the platform; the train shuddered and lurched forward. He got up and went back down the aisle to where Arleigh had been sitting. His newspaper turned out to be a three-day-old copy of the *Casper Intelligencer*. An item at the bottom of the second page caught his eye. It briefly recounted the brazen theft of the money from the Fodder City Miners and Merchants Bank. The last three lines intrigued him.

"Allison and the sole surviving member of his ruthless gang are believed heading for Canada. Law-enforcement officials in the north have been alerted."

Allison's face graced dozens of walls in dozens of stations en route southward, suggesting to Horne that few people were taking seriously the words of the *Casper Intelligencer* reporter. Horne slept all night in his seat, awakening with an agonizing crick in his neck, a foul taste in his mouth, and his body feeling as if he had fallen from a great height onto solid stone. His head ached, his stomach growled and discharged too much acid, his bladder signaled it was preparing to burst. He stood in line for the necessary, fighting the urge to hop from one foot to the other to forestall an accident.

The train pulled into Garden City, Kansas, middle of the afternoon. There he would be changing over to the Atchison, Topeka & Santa Fe only briefly until Bucklin, where he would change again to the Chicago, Rock Island & Gulf. It was a zigzag run all the way down to Texas, time-consuming and indolently slow, but faster than horses direct. The Chicago, Rock Island & Gulf Railroad would take him as far as Stratford in northern Sherman County just over the border. From Stratford he would have to take the stage to tiny Tioga. It was not a prospect that invited; he disliked stagecoaches with a passion. To have to board one at the end of a train ride as exhausting as this one was a discouragingly black prospect. Still, as long as it got him where he had to go . . .

One aspect of the situation was favorable: Allison and Leland riding down, and he was certain they were continuing to, unwilling to risk riding a train, being spotted, and trapped aboard at forty miles an hour, had to be far behind him. Good, it gave him the chance to inspect Tioga. Leland's family must live there, if he had a family. His father's gravestone would be in the cemetery. One thing worried Horne: from the little he knew, from what Perry had overheard, Leland was looking forward to stopping off in Tioga. The question was, would Allison be with him or would he keep going, planning to eventually hook up with Leland again someplace farther south? He was not exactly the soul of patience; it seemed unlikely he would bother to traipse about the little town with Leland while the man immersed himself in nostalgia.

The more Horne thought about it, the dicier it became. Texas really was so big. Looking for a man within its borders, even one as notoriously prominent as Clay Allison, made looking for a needle in a haystack easy. Tioga was the key; even if only Leland stopped off there he would do so planning to catch up with Allison later on. He need only spot Leland, follow him around, and follow him when he left. With any luck at all, he would lead him straight to the crazy man.

To be sure, there was always the possibility that if and when they split up, it would be permanent. Which meant that he'd have to waylay Leland and if necessary beat Allison's destination out of him. That could be a problem. He wasn't very good at beating people; he was, in fact, the next thing to a complete washout. Any reasonably robust twelve-year-old able to handle his fists could lick him. He could swing, he was strong, but a lifelong fear of being hit back always caused him to cringe and even close his eyes as he ducked, thereby destroying the accuracy of his punches. Hitting Arleigh over the head in the dark had been much more demanding on his nervous system and heart than it should have been. By the time he was able to step from behind the stanchion and bring his gun down upon his unsuspecting head, he was practically quaking, sweating furiously, his heart pounding, fear of discovery clutching him by the throat.

Was it just that such situations made him uncomfortable because he put too much thought into them? Or was he an out-and-out coward? He prided himself on never showing cowardice gambling, whatever the game, whoever he came up against. Arleigh Surly in the game at Nutthall and Mann's No. 10 Saloon hadn't frightened him in the least—not at the table, but when he accosted him outside, his knees were on the verge of knocking together before the marshal's timely interruption.

He hoped with all his heart it wouldn't come down to fists or guns with Leland. God forbid it come to either with Allison!

Oklahoma Territory seemed as tall south to north as Texas was broad. The landscape was wearisomely flat and uninteresting. Wheatfields and cattle lands stretched away on both sides. The train crossed the border and pulled into Stratford at ten o'clock at night. He got off and stood on the little platform, taking in all he could see of the town. The Wells, Fargo depot was up the street paralleling the platform to his left. The engine idled, sending intermittent puffs of steam *whooshing* up from its underbelly. People passed him on both sides. He heard a voice behind him.

"Well, look who's here! I thought that was you when we stopped in Anadarko."

He tensed and turned slowly. There, dressed to the nines in clouds of red satin and black velvet, all smiles, radiating charm, extending one gloved hand to grasp his, stood Annie Bowater, alias Prunella Watley.

18

"You look as if you'd seen a ghost," Prunella said in a syrupy tone. "Are you alone? Where's Pericles? The last I saw of the dear man was in a filthy cell in Fodder City."

"He's up in Deadwood lying on a bed of pain. He was very nearly beaten to death by Allison and his friend."

"Goodness gracious, will he be all right?"

"In a couple of months, hopefully. As I say, they did their best to kill him."

"How did it happen?"

"It's a long story and not a very pleasant one. I thought you were in jail."

"I was. Sheriff Coombs sent two deputies over from Sundance to collect me. We started back but never got there."

"What happened?"

"Indians."

"Hogwash! What did you do, bribe them?"

"I didn't offer to, it was all their idea."

"What brings you all the way down here?"

"Distance, dear boy; it lends more than enchantment; the farther I travel, the safer I feel."

"Your wanted posters are all over the landscape," Horne said.

"Allison's got ten times as many. He's the quarry of the moment, nobody cares about little me."

"Where are you heading?" Horne asked.

"Tioga. You've probably never heard of it. It's little

more than a wide place in the road down below Rabbit Ear Creek near the Moore County border. And where are you?"

"South."

"Where south?" She smiled, winked, and waggled a finger. "Chasing them, aren't you? So they've still got my money."

"*Your* money?"

"*The*."

"You were in cahoots with Allison, weren't you, Prunella? You as good as admitted you were that day at the sawmill just before the sheriff and the marshal showed up."

"We had an agreement. It goes without saying he failed to honor it."

"So you're going after him hell-bent for breakfast."

"Crude as that sounds, it's pretty much the case."

"Think you can find him?"

"Do you? You know, it might be wise for us to join forces. Two heads are better than one. And I know this territory."

"I'll pass."

"Why not?"

"For beginners, I don't trust you. I stood there watching you double-cross Perry and try to me. I was against asking you in the first place."

"Shame on you, you bad boy, but I forgive you. Seriously let's get together."

"Let's not."

"Suit yourself. Only I've a much bigger score to settle with Allison than either of you, and you can bet your life I'll catch up with him. Don't let me catch you tagging along behind. You might get caught in the cross-fire."

"Good night, Prunella, and good hunting."

Horne tipped his hat and walked off. He got a room at the Stratford House and for fifty cents extra a plunge bath. He sent a get-well telegram to Perry and enjoyed a late-evening steak dinner at the restaurant across the street from the hotel. He retired at midnight and slept until his seven-thirty call.

The morning stage left for Tioga at nine o'clock, giving him time for a leisurely breakfast. All night long, visions of Prunella in her buckskin outfit with her six-guns buckled on flitted through his head. The woman was one of a kind; Perry had misjudged her badly, much too badly for one who prided himself on his ability to judge character. He hadn't even suspected she was wanted; that alone could well have wrecked the lottery even before the drawing. Had Sheriff Coombs come to town with her wanted poster the day before instead of the day after, there would have been hell to pay.

She had struck a deal with Allison to rob the Miners and Merchants Bank. What in the world ever persuaded her to believe he would do all the work, run all the risk, and end up divvying with her? On the other hand, maybe it had worked out exactly as she'd planned it up to a certain point. Maybe she knew full well he would run out on her after the robbery. Why else would she spend the night before rounding up a gang of her own? They were probably lying in wait somewhere outside of town, and when Allison and his followers failed to show, they went looking for them, eventually picked up their trail, and caught up with them at the sawmill.

All of which was pure conjecture on his part, but it did seem to make sense. When the marshal took her back to Fodder City to jail along with Perry, Allison and Leland were rid of her permanently. They certainly must think they were. The law's arrival was something she hadn't figured on. And she'd taken other risks along the way: setting fire to the mill was only one. Had the outlaws failed to get out, they could have been burned alive and the money with them.

Her offer to join him was more in her own interests than his. She needed him for protection and to help when they found Allison. Having him along, she'd be able to keep an eye on him as well. It was even possible she had ideas about using him for live bait to dangle in front of the crazy man. Whatever she had in her devious mind he wanted no part of it.

He recalled their conversation on the platform the night before. He hadn't told her he, too, was heading for Tioga. He wondered if she knew he knew about the place and Leland's association with it? She had to; why else would he head for Texas?

She was as shrewd as she was devious, and she took great pleasure in manipulating people. She'd manipulated Perry and tossed him squarely into the lap of the law at the sawmill. He'd be damned if he'd give her the chance to manipulate him. Allison was his, and Annie Bowater alias Prunella Watley had better step aside and give him room or by God she'd regret it!

Over the course of the hour and a half from his morning call until the stage left for Tioga, he became so engrossed in theories and suppositions, conjecture and conclusions revolving around Prunella, he overlooked something that should have come to mind the moment he walked away from her the night before.

It didn't dawn on him until he climbed aboard the stage to discover her already in her seat. Keep her guessing as to his destination was impossible.

"Heading for Tioga, I see," she said sweetly.

He grunted and frowned. Five minutes later the driver and shotgun ascended their perch, the whip cracked, the horses snorted, and away lurched the coach.

HOPE YOU ARE FEELING MUCH IMPROVED STOP THINGS LOOKING GOOD DOWN HERE STOP MET OLD FRIEND OF YOURS TONIGHT STOP PRUNIE ASKED ABOUT YOU STOP WILL BE IN TIOGA TOMORROW STOP I KNOW YOUR PRAYERS GO WITH ME

"Damned fool," sputtered Perry.

He was able to sit up. He sat on the edge of the bed,

his face continuing contorted with pain and every part of him aching furiously. Dr. Blue had set his broken left shoulder in an ascending spica bandage and his arm now in a cast was in a sling. His right ankle was also encased in plaster.

"You've got to give him credit for sand," said the doctor.

"Damned fool!"

"You're really worried about him, aren't you? You really care."

"Somebody's got to; he doesn't."

"Who's Prunie?"

"I told you, she's the sharper from Kansas City we hired for the drawing. A confirmed alcoholic with the scruples of a vixen. She'd double-cross her own child if any man were fool enough to father her one."

"If she's so bad, why did you hire her?"

"She was down on her uppers. My charitable urge got the better of my common sense."

"You think she'll double-cross T.G.?"

"If he gives her the chance, the damned fool. If Allison doesn't get him, she will. She's heartless, a traitor to her sex; she should be locked up and the key melted. How the devil she got away from the law this time I can't imagine. She's a snake."

"Whatever she is, she sure bothers the heck out of you. Lie down."

"I'm sick of lying down."

"Doctor's orders." He eased him back down. "How do you feel?"

"What do you think?"

"I'm supposed to ask every once in a while."

"How long do you think before I can get out of here? A week, two?"

"Maybe a couple of months. Providing you go easy and not overdo it, you eat right, get plenty of sleep, don't get upset, think tranquil thoughts. You really can help yourself, you know."

"Bushwah! Hey, are you going out? Get me a paper. Get all the papers. I want to know what's going on with Allison and his friend. We might get lucky; maybe the law will catch up with him before T.G., before that devil in skirts. Maybe, what do you think?"

"It's possible."

"Bushwah, what do you know?"

Prunella's description of Tioga as a wide place in the road was fitting. It was less than half the size of little Stratford, a cluster of buildings along one side of a wide, dusty street and a huge grain elevator opposite. The entire county seemed to be given over to wheat, golden fields rippling with the breeze in every direction on the way down.

Tioga's smallness was discouraging to Horne. So tiny was it, it looked to be all but impossible to steer clear of Prunella in making the limited rounds, but to his surprise, when the stage pulled up in front of the Tioga restaurant and he and the third passenger got out, she remained in her seat.

"Tioga, Prunella."

"I know, dear boy, I can read; I've changed my mind, I'm staying on till Dumas. I've business there I must attend to."

"Oh?"

She smiled, waved, and winked. He stood watching a man and woman climb aboard while the team was changed, then turning, he walked away. Away rumbled the coach. What was she up to? he wondered. Obviously she knew something he didn't. Should he have stayed aboard? Was she going all the way down to Dumas? Or was she just trying to throw him off the track? What business? Was she rounding up another gang? He stopped a man passing.

"I beg your pardon, how far to Dumas?"

"Thirteen, fourteen miles."

Would she come sneaking back after nightfall? And leaving town, wasn't she taking a chance on missing

Allison and Leland? Hardly, it could be another week before they arrived. As far as she knew, nobody else was actively chasing them, and with the kind of money they were carrying, they could stop over wherever they pleased and live it up as long as they liked.

It was all becoming increasingly frustrating. They held all the cards. Except Prunella; she was the joker in the game. She had told him in Stratford she was going on to Tioga, implying that was to be her final destination. What made her change her mind? That he admitted he was going there too?

He glanced about. He suddenly had second thoughts about staying in town. It was just too open, there was too little protection if trouble were to start. On the way down from Stratford the stage had passed an abandoned farm about two miles north of town. The roof of the house, one entire side, and a good portion of the front had been burned. Standing thirty feet away, the barn had escaped unscathed. He could hole up there and wait for them. On their way to town they would have to pass the place; it was the only road in from the north. If he was patient and kept his eyes open, he'd see them. Just as important, Prunella would not see him. If and when she did come back to Tioga with or without another small army, she'd have no idea where he'd gone.

Two doors up the street was a livery stable. He would rent a horse, only later. Right now he'd walk around and get the feel of the town, though from what he could see he wouldn't need to walk far before he'd be out of it. He strolled up the street and down the opposite side past the grain elevator. A hundred yards behind it he noticed a number of headstones, all but buried in the sunburned grass. He walked over to examine them. Without exception they were badly weather-stained, some barely decipherable, most leaning at awkward angles. A typical rural community cemetery, he thought. Henry Murtha, born 1801, died 1872. His wife, Georgianne, outlived him by a year. Alfred Swingle, born 1840, died 1848. Thomas Copperwaite, born 1830, hanged 1870. Leland Bowater, born 1832, hanged 1866.

"Bowater?

"Leland?

"Leland Bowater! Oh, my . . .God!"

19

He stood staring down at the grave marker, his mind whirling, thoughts careening and clashing. Bowater was not a common name, nor was Leland. Prunella Watley alias Annie Bowater . . . Six feet below his feet lay her husband and somewhere to the north her son was riding with Allison.

It wasn't possible. A bird landed on the marker and peered at him. Why not? its eyes asked. He turned about and went back down the side of the elevator to the street and across to a little building displaying a sign: ROOMS TO LET. Why hide out of town? Why not stay, be there to welcome her back from Dumas? Accept her offer, agree to work with her on condition that she level with him. That was a laugh; asking a woman like Prunella to level was like asking the wind to stop.

Some of it he could figure out for himself. She was the Widow Bowater and Leland was her son. She had used his association with Allison to set up the bank robbery; only, like Allison, Leland had double-crossed her. They had together. Running into the ambush at the sawmill, she had known Leland was inside with the others firing at her. It hadn't fazed her; she and her men had counterattacked furiously, in time routing the bank robbers.

The more he thought about it, the less sense it made. He gave it up. She had all the answers; when she came back, he'd get them out of her somehow.

The parlor of the rooming house was the lobby; a rickity-looking jardiniere stand served as the front desk, the guest book open on it. The parlor smelled of corned beef and cabbage and was clearly the lair of one incapable of throwing anything away. Enough furniture, picture, knickknacks, doodads, and dusty memorabilia were in evidence to decorate an entire house. Off to the right, two steps led down to a low-ceilinged room added to the main house. There was a small bar and a few tables; each boasted its own candle in a bottle. The shutters were closed, the room was in darkness. A penciled sign hung from a cord stretching across the entrance. OPEN AT 4 O'CLOCK.

The sound of the front door opening and closing brought a heavy, perspiring, pleasant-faced woman through the beaded curtain at the rear of the parlor.

"I'd like a room."

"Fifty cents, a dollah, dollah and a quahtah?"

"What's the difference?"

"Dollah and a quahtah gets you a front cohnah room, dollah, front room, fifty cents in the back."

"Fifty cents."

"And ten cents extrah foh a sheet and pillow."

"Fine, fine."

She led him upstairs. She had an annoying habit of loudly sucking one tooth; when she wasn't sucking, she hummed to herself. She wore broken-down slippers that slapped her heels at every step, and she walked in a manner that suggested her feet were killing her. She smelled more strongly of corned beef and cabbage than did the parlor, and brought the odor upstairs with them.

The bed was not quite as narrow as a plank; it sagged in the middle, and when Horne sat on it, the tick mattress crunched loudly. The furnishings were not as abundant as those in the parlor, but what there were were depressing. The mirror over the washbasin was clouded; there was a large, dark crack in the basin; the stink of rotten whiskey vied with the landlady's corned beef and cabbage; the window was without either curtains or a shade and both panes displayed large cracks.

Perhaps washing them would have broken them, he thought, which accounted for their griminess.

"I've changed my mind," he said. "I think I'll go for the dollar room."

"They always do," she said, smiling.

It was little better than the fifty-cent room, only larger and with only one cracked windowpane. He could see down into the street. He paid her $2.20 in advance.

"What time does the stage from Dumas get in?"

"Six o'clock. I'll bring you youh sheet and pillow."

She shuffled toward the door. He called after her.

"Can I ask you something? Have you lived here long?"

"All my life."

"Ever hear of a Leland Bowater?"

"Fathah or son?"

"Father. According to his grave marker, he was hanged. What did he do?"

She snickered. "Not much 'cept make trouble, get on evahyone's nehves. He was a prize, that one. Shiftless, thieving, lying, nastiest disposition you evah saw, and a drunk to boot."

"He was a farmer?"

"Some fahmah. Half-plant a crop, then let it go to weed and seed. Too lazy to lift a hoe. Too lazy to mow. Too lazy even to hiah somebody. Only thing he evah did with any regulahity was cook Old Hen."

"Old Hen?"

"Chock beah. Don't you know what chock beah is? You mix blackstrap molasses with watah, yeast, and cohn pone and let it sit and fehment and stink foh twenty-one days. Then you strain it, bottle it, and cook it. Vilest swill in all creation, but it's got a feahsome kick. Guahanteed to rearrange youh innahds pehmanent."

"He was hanged . . ."

"He got in an ahgument with a neighboh ovah wiah."

"That happens."

"With cattle and sheep, not with wheat, not in Shuhman County. He shot the fellow. They hanged him, Bowatah. I was theah. Fuhst and only hanging I evah went to wheah the crowd cheehed when it was ovah. I remembah the fiddlah played 'The Devil's Gone Back to Hell.' Populah man."

"What happened to his son?"

"Don't know. Run away from home."

"His widow?"

"She left Tioga the day aftah the boy. Nevah heahd about eithah since. You hungry? We don't sehve lunch, just suppah. Five o'clock. If youh late, you don't eat."

"Thanks for the warning."

He ate supper and regreted every bite. The corned beef and cabbage was foul; it tasted like it had been marinated in dirty dishwater. The muffins were rocks, the coffee as vile as chock beer was described as being. After supper, shared with four other boarders, he sat in the bar waiting for the stage from Dumas to show. The shutters had been opened promptly at four o'clock and he could see out the front window. He watched the stage arrive and the shotgun rider offer his hand to Prunella as she stepped out. She was the only passenger to get off. He went outside to meet her.

"Get your business all taken care of?" Horne asked.

"You're still here."

"Did you think I wouldn't be?"

He waited in the parlor while she signed for a room, waited while the landlady took her upstairs to show it to her, and presently, he heard a familiar rustling and back down she came.

"I've changed my mind," he said. He lit a Jersey cheroot and drew on it contentedly.

"About what?"

"Joining forces."

He held the front door for her and followed her outside. The air was very still, the crickets sang in the fields, the sun lowering over the Llano Estacado flared a brilliant, vibrant orange, the residents continued to remain indoors. Since he had arrived, he'd yet to see more than two people at a time outside. Even the diminishing sultriness failed to bring them out. He was beginning to think everybody in Tioga was in hiding.

"We can work together if you still want to," he went on, "only I would like a few answers."

She smiled. "You've been to the cemetery, I see."

"Leland's your son."

"Regrettable, but true."

"You made a deal through him with Allison to rob the bank."

"I was stupid to; knowing Leland as I do, it was idiotic."

"I don't understand, out at the sawmill your hired guns could easily have killed him, your own son."

She froze him with a look that seriously questioned his intelligence, then she laughed lightly. "I could only cross my fingers and hope, T.G. It's ironic; as things turned out, he and Allison were the only ones who got away."

"How did you pick up their trail?"

"I didn't. What day is today?"

"Tuesday, Wednesday, I'm not sure."

"The last week in August. It was the last week in August his father murdered Ben Waterbury, our next-door neighbor. He was caught, tried, convicted, hanged, buried; Leland junior ran away; and I left the next day, all in the last week in August. A propitious time of year for our little family, wouldn't you say? Leland always comes back to Tioga this week to visit his father's grave. It's become a ritual; as far as I know, wherever he is, whatever he's doing, he's never failed to come back. He'll come back this year, watch."

"You came down to see him."

She threw back her head and forced hollow laughter. "You're priceless!"

"You plan to kill him? I don't believe that."

"Don't."

He believed it. He became convinced when she proceeded to castigate Leland as a viper in her womb, a "hideous child, totally incorrigible," and an even more reprehensible man.

"As bad as his father was, he was a saint compared to Leland."

"If he's such a monster, why did you make a deal with him up in Fodder City?"

"I didn't, not with him. I just got him to introduce me to Allison."

"What made you think you could depend on either of them to honor the deal?"

"Again I didn't. I just wanted them to do the dirty work. My plan was for them to rob the bank, then we'd waylay them after they left and take away the money. What I really hoped, what would have been ideal, would have been for the posse to catch up with them and retrieve the money, then we in turn would take it from them. Only the marshal delayed until the sheriff joined him, and you know the rest."

"It seems to me your plan was pretty cumbersome. Why even approach Allison? Why not rob the bank yourself? You certainly had enough guns."

"I don't rob banks, it's much too dangerous. I've never tried it, I never would. I always resort to brains over brawn."

"I can't see as any of it was particularly brainy. There was certainly nothing brainy about the shoot-out."

"There wasn't supposed to be one. If the posse had done its job, it would have caught up with them long before the sawmill."

He could see that she was growing annoyed; her plan had been awkward, overly complicated; she knew it and resented his criticizing. It amused him. She was as vain as she was devious, still he had to give her credit, she'd come a long way in the world from sleepy little Tioga. She'd carved out some career for herself, the wanted dodgers and the price on her head notwithstanding. Now she was back to intercept her son and murder him. Incredible. How could she do such a thing to her own flesh and blood, bad as he was?

He couldn't let her. Leland would probably come to town alone; when he was done paying his respects and left, he could lead him straight to Allison. If he never lived to leave, Allison would be lost to him, probably for good.

He could not allow that to happen. He could not stand idly by and let her do her mischief.

She smiled her icy smile. Again she seemed to be reading his thoughts. "If I were you, T.G., I wouldn't get any ideas about interfering."

"In what?"

"You know what I'm talking about."

They found a bench in front of the livery stable; he dusted it with his hanky and they sat.

"Where did you go when you left Tioga?"

"Kansas City. I arrived there with nine cents in my pocket. I got a job in Kimmerlee's Hotel scrubbing floors, making beds, doing the laundry, cleaning up after the filthiest pigs in Christendom. I worked fourteen hours a day seven days a week. I got twelve dollars a week and free room and board. I saved every cent I could. Kimmerlee owned the saloon next door. It was actually more of a gambling casino with liquor. Business was spectacular. He paid off the entire Kansas City police force, from the commissioner on down, to let him operate without interference. And still made a fortune. I cleaned the place up every Monday and Thursday. I got to going over there early to watch the gamblers. Some of the best card mechanics in the business passed through Kimmerlee's: George DeVol, Jonathan Green, Dick Clark, Bill Clemmins. I met your uncle there. What a gallant fellow he was in his younger days: handsome, debonair. I don't know any man I admire more."

Horne suppressed a snicker.

"I began to practice manipulating, shuffling, palming, bottom-dealing. I worked like a Trojan every free minute I could. I got to be very good. Ask Pericles, he'll tell you. I went to work for the house. A year later I went out on my own. I've been freelancing ever since. I mean what I say, T.G., don't try to stop me from dealing with Leland. You might get hurt.

"Why so concerned with his welfare anyway? After what he and Allison did to Pericles, I should think you'd be offering to help, at least cheer me on."

"I don't know as Leland did anything to him."

"He certainly didn't do anything to discourage Allison." She was staring at him. "I see . . . I think I'm beginning to catch on. You don't want Leland killed, you want him to leave here alive, you think he'll lead you to Clay."

"That's part of it."

"That's all of it. Shame on you, you're being as single-minded about Allison as I am about Leland. But seriously and for the last time, don't get in my way."

"You're already wanted. Why add murder? Why make things worse than they already are?"

"Be a good boy and let me worry about that."

With this she got up and walked away.

He went inside the livery stable to rent a horse. If he could intercept Leland north of town, he could warn him.

And save the useless scoundrel's miserable life . . .

20

On his way out to the abandoned farmhouse, where he planned to stop Leland, it crossed Horne's mind that in his entire conversation with Annie-Prunella, neither of them had said anything about the stolen money since its theft. Now that he thought about it, he could see no possible way that she could know he had found and returned the lion's share, and that all Allison and Leland were carrying now was the $120,000, or what was left of it. Knowing her, she wanted the money as badly as she professed to want Leland's hide . . . More. And she'd spent the better part of an hour the previous evening deliberately confusing him. If he were to team up with her, he'd wind up holding the short end. The woman was a unique piece of work; the best thing he could do for himself would be to stay away from her.

He had brought along food and water and two bottles of a domestic brandy he had never heard of before and had yet to sample. He was planning on at least a two-day vigil. It seemed unlikely that they or Leland alone would be traveling by night. With all that money they'd be living it up after sundown. How far down had they come? he wondered. Through the Oklahoma Panhandle and over the border? Probably not yet. It was less than forty miles through the Panhandle, with the most logical stopover in Boise City, the only community of any size in Cimarron County. If they did stop there, they'd be starting out middle of the morning, sleeping late after a night of carousing. They could be across the border, through Stratford, and approaching any time after two in the afternoon.

They could also still be dawdling somewhere in Kansas.

To his dismay, the barn smelled of manure, not strong enough to make his eyes water, just strong enough to arouse his disgust. He tied the mare in the barn and, bringing his food with him, went around back of the house and inside. The fire had destroyed more of the place than was visible from the front. The flames had taken away most of the roof. He sat in the parlor in a rocking chair surrounded by charred timbers, the cloudless blue sky overhead, and ate one of his three ham sandwiches. He also tried the brandy. It was not nearly as foul as he imagined it would be, but it was watery.

At ten o'clock a stagecoach passed heading north. At ten-fifteen two hay wagons passed in tandem, heading toward Tioga. He went out to the barn to see to the horse. Holding his nose with his handkerchief, he wandered about and found half a barrel of oats. He found a bucket, filled it, and set it in front of the horse. He was petting her and talking soothingly when the sound of hooves came drifting through the partially opened door. He closed it to a slit and looked out. Five riders. In the lead was a familiar figure in mule-skinner buckskins and a wide-brimmed stetson. He could make out one of her two ivory grip Peacemakers and on the far side of her horse a rifle stock angled upward.

"Oh, my God . . ."

He quickly saddled the horse, started for the house to collect his food, changed his mind, threw open the barn door, and rode off after them. Why, he wondered, had he reacted with surprise? He'd already figured what the object of her trip to Dumas was the day before: her "business" there had been to hire four guns.

T.G. stayed a safe distance behind their dust, and dusty the road was, sending up a cloud that completely obscured them from his sight. And him from theirs, in case they looked back. She would continue north until she sighted Leland and Allison, however long it took her. She'd set up her ambush, get the drop on them, kill them, and then relieve them of their money. She had no more liking for shoot-outs than robbing banks she made no secret of her distaste for the one at the sawmill.

Horne chuckled. She was in for a surprise: the half million had dwindled to little more than a hundred thousand. Not exactly a widow's mite, but a far cry from what she expected. Would she really shoot Leland? Or was that all noise designed to divert his attention from her real purpose? Time will tell, he thought.

The golden landscape waved appreciation to the sun. In the distance Stratford Loomed with its flimsy frame store buildings and brick-and-stucco houses sitting basking in the sun. Not a wisp of cloud smudged the brilliant sky. T.G. lagged farther behind as they slowed and passed through town.

He thought about Perry. He would live, thanks to Dr. Blue and his own fierce, even ferocious will to survive. But would he ever be the same? Old bones knit slowly, if at all; from now on every morning when he awoke, his body would remind him of Clay Allison and the crazy man's face would imprint itself on the screen of his imagination. Would he heal perfectly or would he be crippled? Dr. Blue refused to make a prediction. There was no way he could. His primary job at the moment, now that the bleeding was stopped and all the bones set, was holding his patient down, keeping him reined to prevent him from hurting himself or interfering with his healing. Lying helpless in distant Deadwood with nothing to do but suffer and think, Perry would be conjuring up all sorts of black thoughts. He no doubt already had him lying facedown in a Texas ditch with four bullets in his back. Letting his good sense be abducted by his fancy was not the best thing Perry could do for himself. Dr. Blue would try to dispel his concern with all sorts of optimistic supposition, but Perry would shut out his voice.

Too bad there was no telegraph office in Tioga. He could have sent him a wire reassuring him. He couldn't risk stopping long enough in Stratford to send one; he could too easily lose Prunella and her gang.

Visualizing Perry captive of his pain, seeing him suffer in his mind's eye, stoked Horne's fury against Allison anew. He was now past caring what happened to Leland and whether or not his mother would carry out her threat. Neither one mattered, nor was the money important any longer. Allison was all. Horne had never killed a man; on rare occasions he'd shot in self-defense, but deliberately shooting to kill would be a new experience for him. There was always a first time, especially in the West, where practically everybody carried weapons. Reflecting on this, he was surprised that it had taken him this long, he'd gotten this old without killing.

Could he do it? When he got Allison face to face, would he be able to? If anything made him hesitate, he need only think of Perry.

Two miles north of Stratford Prunella and her hirelings swerved off the road. There were no trees, but a long ledge of sandstone protruded from the flat ground surrounding it, and it was to this ledge that they made their way. They dismounted, pulled their horses down, and hid.

Horne had pulled up to watch. He then swung about and cantered back toward Stratford. Now that they had stopped, when their dust settled, one or another might look back and see him. The road was straight as wire: no trees, no boulders of any size to block out sight of him, nothing but wheat and their ledge.

He cut off the road into a wheatfield; he got his horse down and waited. He could see nothing. He could hear only the breeze swishing softly through the wheat crowns.

He strained to listen. Growing impatient, he crept back up onto the road. Two riders were coming, twin black smudges against the sky. On they came at a lope. He held his breath as they passed the ledge and the waiting ambush. He drew back into the field and watched them pass him: two old men; they looked like brothers. They were arguing and seemed entirely oblivious of their surroundings. Seconds later they were out of sight. Prunella and her men, meanwhile, had gotten back onto the road. He let them move out, then followed.

Late in the afternoon they forded Beaver Creek and crossed the border; a crudely lettered sign was the only evidence that Texas stopped and the Oklahoma Panhandle began. They came to a fork in the road. An arrow sign pointed the way to Boise City to the left. The sun was beginning to lower, but it would be at least three hours before it vanished completely. Slender slate clouds trafficked the distant horizon.

Would they lead him all the way to Boise City? he wondered. Would Leland and Allison be coming through there? The more he thought about it, the less likely it seemed. Coming straight down from the north would bring them through eastern Colorado; western Kansas, through the Smoky Hills, was a far more inviting route: more and bigger towns, more good-time stopovers, more gambling, drink, women . . .

Would the two outlaws pass them on their right so far away they'd never see them? Possibly. The right fork of the road could no longer be seen. They had been climbing onto a lofty tableland. The terrain changed dramatically. Canyons, buttes, and mesas appeared; this was the beginning of the Great Plains region east of the Rocky Mountains.

He was beginning to worry in earnest. What if they had lost the two by turning off? What if the chase was all over and Prunella didn't even realize it? Why should he even follow them? What did she know that he didn't?

About an hour before the sun set, his fears vanished. He watched as Prunella and her men again veered off the road, this time to their left, taking up positions behind a convenient scattering of boulders. Far up the road a column of dust rose. Two riders showed briefly, then disappeared behind the rocks. Horne cut off the road to the right, swinging wide and coming back behind the concealment of an outcropping just up the way from where Prunella and her men waited. From his position he could see them strung out behind their boulders, Prunella about fifteen feet ahead of the others. She had her .45 out, cocked and ready. Her exression was that of one who had already killed her nemy, was already savoring the satisfaction.

The second he recognized Leland and Allison approaching, Horne tensed. Should he warn them? If he lid, Prunella and her men would surely turn their guns n him. If he did not, the two outlaws would ride into a ail of bullets. The stage was set before him: the ambush waited, pistols and rifles readied to pour death.

Leland and the money be damned, he thought. He ould not let Allison be killed. Not by a stranger's hand, ot by any hand but his. And he wanted to face him, nake and hold eye contact, accuse him, attack him, eat him to a pulp, break every bone in his worthless ody!

He drew his .45 and fired in the air. As one, the mbushers turned toward him, freezing momentarily. He ducked and held his breath. The approaching outlaws stopped so abruptly they were nearly thrown. When next he looked, they were whirling about in confusion as Prunella and her men recovered from their surprise and opened fire. In that brief moment of hesitation Leland had gotten his gun out; he emptied it, firing wildly. Horne watched in astonishment as Prunella screamed, rose to her feet, dropped both hands still grasping her guns, gaped, and toppled over.

Leland whooped. His elation was short-lived. He had turned to ride off back the way they'd come. As Horne shifted his eyes from Prunella to him, Leland was hit squarely between the shoulder blades. He flinched at the impact, roared, and lifted his elbows high to either side, as if trying to force the slug from his spine. Then down he fell, his hat flying off, one foot catching in a stirrup. His horse dragged him a few yards, stopped, pawed the ground, and tossed its head.

Wholly absorbed by the sight, standing half-crouched, Horne failed to notice his own horse wander from behind her cover. Two rifles cracked. She was hit in the chest; she turned toward him, her eyes rounding; she whinnied plantively, her forelegs buckled, and down she went, rolling on her side, dead.

With all eyes briefly on Leland, Allison had made i to cover. He now took off in a hail of fire, swerving thi way and that as he fled. The scattered boulders helpe shield him and he opened up a good hundred yard between himself and the ambushers before they coul get clear sight of him again. One was shouting, cursing ordering the others to mount. Away they flew, takin Prunella's horse with them, thundering past her motionless body without so much as a quick glance dow at it.

Allison had all the lead he needed on them, Horn decided; in this terrain he could find a hundred place to hide; he probably wouldn't bother; he'd probabl continue to leg it north until he shed them.

Horne muttered and seethed. The swiftness and violence of the brief action had rooted him where he stood. Leland lay where he had fallen, his ankle still caught in the stirrup. His horse stood stock-still. Horne ran toward it. He was almost up to it, his gun holstered, both hands out-stretched, preparing to rump-vault onto its back when Leland moved. He stopped short and watched him come to life, extricate his ankle, prop himself with his stiffened right arm, struggle to push himself fully upright.

Horne helped him to a sitting position. "Where's he heading, Leland?"

"Tilly . . . What the . . . ?"

"Tell me, where were you two heading?"

"Ti . . . oga . . ."

"You. What about him?"

"I'm dying. Jesus, it hurts."

"Where?"

"I'm all fillin' up with blood inside. I got her, though, didn't I? Got her 'fore . . . 'fore she got me."

His eyes were rapidly glazing; Horne had to hold him to keep him from falling over; his arms around him, he could feel the life seeping from him.

"Where's Allison heading? Where were you going to meet him after Tioga? Where? Tell me!"

"Way . . ."

"Away where?"

"Co."

"Coe? Leland . . . Leland!"

Leland opened his mouth, but no further words came out. He drew in a breath and with great effort lifted his head. He leered up at him, his head fell, his body slumped.

Horne eased him to the ground. "Leland . . ."

It was no use.

"Coe? Away? Way? Waco? Waco! Yes, yes, yes, yes . . ."

The warm glow of relief filled his chest; he closed Leland's eyes and went back to Prunella. She lay awkwardly twisted, as if someone had impishly set her arms, legs, and head askew. She stared sightlessly, the weight of the flesh around her crimsoned mouth pulling her lips back, exposing her teeth in a sardonic grin.

If she could speak, she would be laughing, he mused. In triumph? He glanced back at Leland.

He closed her eyes. He looked a slow circle around him. Not a sign of a soul. Second thoughts assailed him. Should he have ignored Leland and gone after Allison? No. Had he done so and lost him, it would probably be for good, or until the next time he got into dutch and into the newspapers. No, Leland knew where he was heading and had lived just long enough to tell him.

But as he was dying, why had he leered at him the way he did? He couldn't have lied; with his last breath he couldn't have deliberately deceived him. A dying man always told the truth.

"So they say. That's what they say. You wouldn't lie, would you, Leland? Would you?"

21

Waco nested in the wide valley of the Brazos River, a big green bowl rimmed about by the hills of the Balcones Escarpment. The valley was a fertile farming region. During Reconstruction, settlers arrived in droves from the ruined southern states, seeking a new life. Cattle moved up the trails toward northern markets. On January 6, 1870, a suspension bridge replaced the twenty-one-year-old ferry. It was the only bridge across the Brazos, and travelers journeying westward swarmed through the town. From a dignified, live-oak-shaded village, steeped in the traditions of the South, Waco became a rip-roaring frontier town, displaying false-front hotels and notorious gambling halls. Great herds of cattle, wagons piled high with hides, cotton, and wheat, and long freighting trains lumbered across the bridge. Loose-living, rampaging cowboys and lawless buffalo hunters infested the town, attracting parasites from all over the state.

Horne stood at the bar in Donegan's Saloon and Gambling Casino across the street from Waco's most popular attraction, the Star Variety Theater. The town's wide-open reputation was everywhere in evidence, he reflected, looking around. Waco was overcrowded, Waco was loud, and the class of humanity it catered to was a generous cut below Fodder City's. By comparison, Waco made Deadwood look downright genteel.

If Clay Allison were coming to town, he would feel right at home. Arriving two hours before, Horne had searched for him from one end of town to the other, but as yet there was no sign of him.

Why Waco? he wondered. What was the lure? Safety in numbers of his kind? From what he could see at the moment, half the visitors were bad medicine uncomplainingly swallowed by the locals. Law and order were conspicuously absent. Was it a woman who was bringing him to town? What did it matter what it was as long as he showed up?

Horne had retrieved the rented saddle from the rented horse and ridden Leland's horse back to Tioga. The stableman had grudgingly accepted it in place of the mare. Horne departed for Waco on the first of a series of stages. He left with no regrets over not staying at the scene of the shoot-out to bury mother and son. He had nothing to dig with; besides, someone would surely pass that way and see to them before the buzzards arrived, bringing their insatiable appetites.

Horne sipped his whiskey and wondered why he always seemed to be ahead of the man he was after. Doubtless because Allison was in no hurry. Still, it didn't make Horne's job any easier. He looked about Donegan's. He had seen the place five hundred times in five hundred towns border to border, larger and smaller, noisier, but the same faces, the identical sounds: the click of the roulette ball, the rattle of the dice in the chuck-a-luck cage, the slap of cards, the same songs suffering at the hands of the same mediocre piano players, the clink of glasses, the hammer of bottles, the laughter, the grumbling, the swearing, the same spirited discussions. And the smell always the same. He peered through the dirty window at the Star Variety Theater across the street. In wandering about town looking for Allison, he had stopped to look inside. The evening performance was scheduled for eight, two hours hence. Lotta Crabtree was starring in *Under the Gaslight*.

Getting off the stage, he had bought two newspapers, a week-old copy of the *Austin Statesman* and a more recent edition of the *Galveston News*. Neither made any mention of Allison and his exploits. In the days since Deadwood the crazy man had become old news, pushed into obscurity by other events. Time passing was his most dependable ally, reflected Horne ruefully. The only thing left keeping him before the public eye was his wanted dodger, and even that would surely start its way down the pile, when another of his stripe took the spotlight.

He had stopped earlier at the Western Union office to send a wire to Perry. He had inquired about his recovery. Finishing his drink, he left Donegan's, heading for Western Union hopeful that a reply had come in. One had. It was from Dr. Blue.

> HES COMING ALONG BUT DONT XPECT
> OVERNIGHT MIRACLES STOP I MEASURE
> HIS RECOVERY BY STEADY INCREASE
> IN HIS GRUMBLING AND FAULT FINDING
> STOP THE DAY WILL COME WHEN HE
> WILL LOSE HIS TEMPER STOP WILL
> SURELY COINCIDE WITH COMPLETE
> RESTORATION STOP ABSOLUTELY
> INCORRIGIBLE PATIENT OBMD

He smiled. "Good. Excellent."

The lady who had replaced the man behind the counter since his last visit was young and pretty, but one had to look close to perceive it. Her glistening black hair was pulled back severely in a tight bun; she wore eyeglasses with nickel frames, and no makeup other than a faint blush of lipstick, without which she would have looked pale as a sheet. He optimistically assumed that she had a lovely figure, but whatever she had was well concealed under a frumpy dress that looked to be the taste of a woman three times her age. She worked conscientiously to keep her pretty little nose in the air, her eyes away from his, her chin up, and her lips pursed disdainfully. Had he not known better, he would have imagined she was sniffing something disagreeable. The only odor he could identify in the office was his Jersey cheroot as he drew it under his nose, preparatory to lighting up.

"No smoking."

"Oh, sorry."

"Will there be a reply?"

"No. No, thank you."

He wondered if her efforts at aloofness were designed as a defense against Waco's ill-mannered majority. What was she doing there anyway? She no more fit its rascally image than a buzzard fit a birdbath. He was staring at her busily writing, then jamming her pencil into her bun. He caught himself too late.

She stared sternly. "Yes?"

"I . . ."

"Is there anything else?"

"No. No, thank you."

"Very well."

He left. What ailed her, for pity's sakes? Why so stony cold, contemptuous, determinedly distant? He looked back inside. She was watching him. She didn't gesture, didn't move a finger, did nothing whatsoever to summon him back in, but her expression insisted he return. He went back inside.

"Forgive me if I was rude," she said.

"You weren't."

"I was."

"Not really. You were preoccupied, I was dawdling."

"My name is Prunella." He started and resisted the urge to swallow. "Prunella Golightly."

He tipped his hat. "Delighted to meet you, Miss Golightly."

"Prunella."

"Prunella."

"And you're Mr. Horne."

"I go by my initials, T.G."

"T.G. You're new in town."

"I just got here a couple hours ago. Here on business."

"Where are you staying?"

"The Lone Star."

"Best place in town."

"It seems comfortable."

Under all the frills and flounces and furbelows he envisioned massive, exquisitely sculptured breasts, and beneath them a smooth, pink, concave stomach and below that a gleaming, jet-black vee wherein lurked soft, pink, inviting lips. Ah, the stuff that daydreams are made of, he mused longingly.

She smiled for the first time; to his delight her face wasn't pretty, it was beautiful.

"Enjoy your stay."

"I shall, I hope."

Horne went back to the hotel. He had taken a front room overlooking the street and a row of saloons uninterrupted by any store or other types of business establishments. Drinking, gambling, and carousing seemed to be Waco's only enterprise. He was tired. He stripped off his shirt and undershirt and washed. The nearly 450-mile trip had consumed better than four days; it had seemed like a month, but as yet no train reached this far south and riding a horse that long and that far was out of the question. At that, he had apparently beaten Allison to town, if indeed he was coming.

Horne resolved not to start worrying for at least another day. He dried himself and put on a clean shirt. He stood at the mirror combing his hair. A light knock sounded. He went to the door.

"Yes?"

There was no response; the knock was repeated.

He unbolted and opened the door. "Miss Golightly . . ."

"Prunella."

"Prunella. Ah . . . Won't you come in?"

She had started in before he could finish his invitation. She threw a cursory glance about the room, glided past him to the bed, and tested it with one hand. He closed the door.

"My goodness, this is a pleasant surprise."

She said nothing. Reaching into her reticule, she brought out a small bottle, setting it on the dresser. It looked like shampoo. She did not comment on it. She approached him and stood facing him, less than six inches separating their noses. She removed her glasses and set them beside the bottle. She unpinned her hair, letting it billow down in glistening waves; she unfastened the button at her throat; she seized his head and pressed her lips hard against his, so hard his one slightly misaligned incisor dug deep into his bottom lip, threatening to crack it. She let him go, turned her back, and starting at the top, began undoing her buttons.

"Yes . . . a pleasant surprise."

She said nothing. He silently counted the buttons. At twelve her naked back appeared fully; at sixteen, the crack of her buttocks. She did not wear a stitch of underclothing. The bottom, twenty-second button, was unfastened, and down fell her dress, frills, flounces, and furbelows. Leaving it where it lay, she stepped out and turned to face him. He gasped audibly. He began to tingle all over. In the office his imagination, speculating on what she looked like under her old lady's dress, he now realized he had badly underestimated her. Her figure was incredible; she knew it. His ill-concealed reaction failed to alter in the slightest her impassive expression. Again she kissed him, this time much more tenderly, working her lips warmly against his, at the same time pressing against him.

Releasing him and stepping back, she set about undressing him.

"A wonderful surprise . . . really . . ."

Nothing.

In sixty seconds he was as naked as she, with his organ fully erect. She positioned him at the foot of the bed and oiled him down with the contents of the bottle, saving the last of it to rub herself down. Then, getting onto the bed on her knees, she began to lick. His tingling was turning into fire, flames from inside searing every part of it. On she lapped and laved and licked, lathering his cock. He stood with trembling hands on her shoulders, looking down at her bobbing head. Tremor after tremor passed downward through his body.

He was coming. He stiffened and swallowed, sealing his eyes, every bone in his body liquefying. He came, firing again and again, and still she sucked, drawing the life and the last drop from him. Until a second erection began. Sucking, sucking, stiffening him. Harder, harder, rising, throbbing . . .

She freed her mouth and gazed up at him, her eyes glazed. She lay back upon the bed, pushing herself up it with her heels, and gestured him to mount her, holding her lips apart to accept him. He eased into her and began slow, deep, rhythmic thrusts, with each pull nearly leaving her vagina. She smiled approvingly and upthrust her hips to receive him.

They came as one; she sucked in a breath and held it; he squinched his eyes and died a little as their explosions clashed. And still they continued, in and out, gradually decending from the heights, easing comfortably down, down until the final thrust and buck.

Slowly they separated. No sooner was she free than up she jumped. Reaching into her reticule, she brought out a folded paper, a rubber stamp and ink pad.

"What's that?" he asked.

"Read it." They were her first words since entering the room.

He unfolded the paper. It was a bill "for services rendered." The fee was two dollars.

"Two?"

She nodded. He shrugged. He got out his wallet and paid her.

"Thank you."

She took the bill from him, tore off the bottom part, laid it on the dresser, and inking her stamp, stamped it "paid" and gave it back to him.

"Your receipt."

"Ah . . . thank you."

They got dressed. He was buttoning his shirt when a

clamor erupted in the street below. Together they went to the window. Hordes of people milled about, lights blazed, a gun was fired, then another. Shades of Deadwood, he thought. A large hay wagon was parked in the middle of the street. A man dressed as a clown was sitting in the bed beating a huge drum. On it was the legend: JUDGE GILES FOR MAYOR: HONESTY, INTEGRITY, SOBRIETY.

The candidate lifted his considerable bulk into the wagon and stood waving both meaty hands as his audience began to assemble. But it wasn't the judge or those he was gathering that caught Horne's eye. It was a familiar figure walking up the sidewalk under the connecting overhangs, carrying his saddlebags over his shoulder, turning, pushing through the batwing doors of the Broken Spur.

22

He looked like the front half of a bull, all massive chest with his cask head jammed between his shoulders. He was completely bald, his expression was determinedly threatening, and his hand was out. "Check your iron, pilgrim."

Horne hesitated. "How come? I didn't have to in Donegan's this afternoon."

"Every plathe maketh you at night. Thath the kind of town thith ith."

He readied a two-part tag. Horne unbuckled and handed him his belt with his two .45s and was given his tag.

"And that derringer or whatever it ith bulgin' your vetht there."

Horne sighed and complied.

"Ith that all, you don't have a knife, do you?"

Horne surrendered his dagger-mounted knuckleduster.

The man chuckled. "You thure are loaded for bear. That it?"

Horne nodded, confident that he wouldn't search him and find the Barns in his right boot. He started down the bar. Three faro games were going on against the wall on the right. In the far corner a number of players crowded around the roulette table. There were two poker games going on against the rear wall. He espied Allison next to the back door, his saddlebags still draped over his shoulder. He was playing with three others. Horne started toward him. He was six steps from the table when Allison looked up from his cards. A grin of recognition spread across his pale face.

"Will you look who's here? If it ain't Mr. Tilly in the flesh. What in hell you doin' way down here? Last I seen o' you was at the sawmill up in the Black Hills. Come over here. Come say hello to Bert, Evelyn, and Jake Cameron. Boys, this here is Mr. Tilly; he's a banker, when he's not playing hostage, that is. Ha ha."

The three nodded without looking up, obviously not interested in socializing.

"What's the bet?"

"Five bucks to you, Clay," Bert said.

All three looked very much alike, beetle-browed with belligerent expressions, overly generous lower lips, and jutting jaws. Jake was missing a good part of his left ear. Clay met the bet and raised.

"Ten bucks to play, boys. Hey, Tilly, come sit aside me. We got some catching up to do, you an' me. You play poker?"

"Some."

"Got any money? Must have some; you didn't get all the way down here on your looks, right? Ha."

"I'm calling, Clay," Bert said. "What you got?"

"Three little sixes."

"Beats me."

Clay raked in the pot.

"It's five bucks an' ten, Tilly, you can 'ford that. Evelyn, you're the bank, sell my friend here some chips."

Horne was sitting so close to him his upper right arm came in contact with the saddlebags. In them had to be the $120,000, or what was left of it. It had to be most of it. It was a comfort to know too that Allison hadn't spotted him at the shoot-out. At that, there was no way he could have; he'd been very careful not to show himself during the actual shooting. It wasn't his quarrel; no reason to give either side an additional target.

"What happened to Leland?" he asked.

"Bowater? Oh, him and me split up. Hey, what

happened to the old man, you know, Mr. No Name. What was his name, anyhow?"

"Youngquist."

"Ha, no wonder he wouldn't tell me. That's a funny name. Youngquist, old quist. Where'd he get to?"

"He ran into a buzz saw up in Deadwood. He was killed."

"You don't say. Ain't that a shame."

Allison snickered and Horne hated him a little more. Yes, unquestionably, given the opportunity, he could kill him . . . slowly, painfully. His cries would be music; he looked forward to it. But it couldn't be in front of a crowd. Somehow he'd have to get him off alone, get the drop on him.

No, first beat him up. Beat him as no man had ever beaten any other on God's green earth. Break him into dice-sized pieces inside the sack of his skin while every drop of his miserable blood seeped out of him. Beat him! Beat him! Beat him!

"You say somethin', Tilly?"

"No."

"I thought I saw your lips moving. What are you doin' down here?"

"Business for the Banking Commission."

"Hear that, boys? Didn't I tell you he was a banker?"

"Who gives a shit?" said Jake. "Let's play cards. Your deal, Tilly."

Horne had him in his corner; Allison seemed actually delighted to see him again. How he'd love to put him through the wringer and take a bundle from him, but why deliberately antagonize him? It would be utterly stupid.

He got no cards the first four hands. In the fifth round, a game of draw, he caught three jacks on the deal and, holding a kicker in the manner of a rank amateur—a queen—drew a useless seven. One by one the Cameron brothers dropped out, leaving him and Allison toe to toe. Allison insisted on raising and reraising;

Horne finally folded. At the brothers' loud insistence Allison showed his winning hand, aces over threes.

"You sure scared me," said Horne. "I dropped out with three jacks."

He fished them out of the discards and showed them. Allison laughed uproariously. Horne had lost forty dollars on the one hand. In the hand following, Jake filled an inside straight and beat Allison's three queens. He exploded, loudly, vilely cursing Jake's luck, shooting to his feet, seizing the edge of the table and flipping it chips, cards, money, and all into the winner's lap.

"This game shits," he boomed. "Come on, Tilly, we're gettin' outta here."

"I checked my gun . . ." began Horne.

"To hell with it. Pick it up later. Let's go!"

"What the hell you do that for, Clay?" Jake snarled.

"You crazy?" Bert rasped.

Allison froze. "Who you callin' crazy, you ugly bastard! Huh? Who? Who?"

"That's a helluva thing to do," responded Bert, softening his tone. "You've mixed up all the money."

"To hell with the money! Nickels an' dimes, asshole; stupid, penny-pinchin' son of a bitch! Come on, Tilly."

A crowd was gathering.

Allison grabbed Horne by the arm and pulled him out the door. He was livid, his face purpling, nostrils flaring, eyes firing. "The nerve o' that son of a bitch callin' me crazy!" He stopped short. "I gotta mind to go back an' smash his ugly face in."

"Don't do it, Clay."

"Penny-pinchin' sons o' bitches, that's what all them Camerons are."

The night was seasonably hot, the air close. A full moon hung overhead, painting the surrounding area in ghostly tints. The street noises out front were muffled, even the pistol shots. A dog yapped in the distance, encouraging a coyote to bay mournfully. The back door of the Broken Spur was pulled shut, the vertical rectangle of yellow light vanishing.

They walked about twenty yards, Allison continuing to fume and rant. He stopped abruptly, threw down his saddlebags, and glared fiercely. "I'm goin' back there."

"No you're not!"

"The hell I'm not! Who's gonna stop me?"

Horne swung, slamming him full in the gut. His fist felt as if it were penetrating to within an inch of his backbone. It felt good, great, propelled as it was by pure hatred. It warmed Horne all over.

It doubled Allison, his breath whooshing from him. "Ahhh . . ." He straightened slowly. When his face came up, on it was gaping disbelief. "You hit me."

Horne smashed his gape. The instant he made contact, satisfaction exploded in his knuckles, warm and surging back through his fist, his wrist up his arm to his shoulder. Beautiful! Magnificent! An extraordinary feeling! He aimed his left to follow up, but Allison recovered too quickly; up came his right arm, warding it off, sending his fist harmlessly over his shoulder.

Up came Allison's left, ramming him in the temple, setting him teetering to the left on one foot, nearly toppling. A huge bell clanged in his head, splitting his eardrums and lifting his pate straight upward. The ringing echoed and echoed, the world whirled. Allison followed up with a wild flurry of punches, a windmill of fists hammering, glancing off, missing his upper body and face. For ten interminable seconds before he could regain his bearings, it rained knuckles. Instinctively, wholly unaware he was throwing the punch, his right drove forward, hammering Allison's gut a second time, slightly higher, three fingers above his navel. Again he grunted and folded, so tightly his chest nearly touched his knees.

Recovering from his dizziness, Horne straightened and brought up his right knee, pounding Allison full in the face before he could lift it above the horizontal. A loud, sickening squishing sound was followed by the audible cracking of gristle. Allison cursed, gagged, and staggered back. He straightened slowly, bringing his ace back into view, revealing his nose smashed flat against it, blood spurting from his nostrils, draping his mouth and chin. Fists came flying at Horne; for a long moment he imagined not one but four people were attacking him. He ducked and brought both his fists up as one, catching Allison squarely under the chin, lifting it, cracking it loudly at the hinges, driving his lower teeth hard against his uppers and shattering them.

"Eeeeyaaaa!"

His eyes blazed. "I'll kill . . . kill . . . you."

A cloud passed over the moon, quenching its light, plunging the combatants into darkness. Two figures were approaching. Three more appeared, coming from the opposite direction. Allison's scream had opened back doors up and down the line; people emerged. The five men formed a circle around the two, their backs to them, legs spread apart, walling them in.

Horne was hurting: his face felt pounded to a pulp, his right shoulder ached furiously, and his chest rang with pain behind his battered ribs. But he could see that Allison was weakening rapidly, having lost a great deal of blood and still spitting teeth. His body may have been giving out, but his heart was still very much in the fight; in him was the raw fury of a wounded wolf. In his wild eyes Horne could see that he was prepared to fight to the death if need be, slam and hammer, gouge and rip, bite, butt, kick, knee, stomp, attack, attack . . .

Allison lowered his head, blood dripping from his mouth, and bulled forward. Horne swung sideways out of his path and, as he hurtled by, brought both fists pile-driving down on his neck. Allison's head nearly struck the ground; he dropped to his knees, fell on his side, rolled over, and raised himself slowly on all fours. Horne drew back his right leg, willed it full of power, and kicked Allison full in the ribs, cracking them loudly, triggering a harrowing scream.

"Kill . . . kill . . . kill you."

Horne lifted his fists and with every ounce of strength left in him brought them down on the back of Clay's head, snapping it down to his breastbone. Down he fell again, breathing huskily through the bloody slit of his mouth. His lower face was completely bloodied, his nose squashed and spread twice normal size, and his eyes rolled with agony. His lips moved, but nothing came out. Horne leaned over him.

The five men circling them remained stock-still. Since they had taken up their positions, not a face turned, not an eye looked toward them. Horne pulled up his pantleg, drew his Barns, confirmed it was loaded, aimed at Allison's face, cocked, and pulled the trigger.

Tried to, struggled to . . . but his finger refused to answer the command of his brain. It seemed paralyzed. He grunted, straining to draw it back, but could not move it. Slipping his left-hand index finger behind it, he strained again, but could not fire. His hand trembled, his arm, his entire upper body. It was useless. The foggy eyes stared upward at him. The lips moved around the bloody hole, the breath rasped forth.

A voice spoke behind Horne. "Don't . . ."

Another spoke. "His is the spirit of the unclean devil, but thou shalt not kill."

Horne lowered his arm slowly. The pistol dropped from his hand.

23

In the company of the five clergymen Horne staggered back to his hotel and was helped up to his room. They stood patiently waiting as he washed his face and cleared the cobwebs and dulled his various aches and pains with a tumbler of the contents of a bottle offered him by Father Dunphy. Rev. Miller had brought along Allison's saddlebags. They were upended over the bed. Out fell four biscuits, a half-filled box of Remington Arms cartridges, a brand-new Remington Frontier .44 with cosmoline still in the barrel, a half filled bottle of Cooperman's sour mash whiskey, a tightly rolled-up wanted poster offering "$5,000 reward for information leading to the arrest and conviction of Clay Allison," a blurred and yellowed tintype of a round-faced woman with a beguiling smile and a small boy on her lap who looked very much like Allison, newspaper clippings detailing his exploits (one of them four years old), a nearly empty tin of Peaberry mocha coffee, a coffeepot, a tin cup, a small cast-iron fry pan, a knife with the name Ed Haas carved in the hilt and dried blood caking two-thirds of the blood channel, a nearly full bottle of Dr. Schenck's Fix Laxative, four stogies, a box of parlor matches, a half-used roll of toilet paper, a metal mirror with the initials C.A. scratched on the back, a yellowed and fray-edged medical discharge from the army of the CSA for C. Allison, Private, attached to the Tennessee Light Artillery, a tintype of Allison looking as dour and disdainful as ever, sitting holding one crutch with the other lying across his left leg set across his right, his left foot heavily bandaged. There was a packet of Armbruster needles and a spool of thread, there were maps of all the Plains states with bank sites penciled in. There were two pair of dice and a pack of Bicycles, a spade bit, a rabbit's foot, a Waterbury watch with a diagonal crack across the face, a silver ring bearing the initials J.F., a three-blade stag-handle knife, a Wostenholm pipe razor, and ninety dollars in ten-dollar bills.

"Ninety dollars!" bawled Horne. "What happened to the hundred and twenty thousand?"

Rev. Miller looked even more startled than the others. "He took a hundred and twenty thousand dollars from the bishop?"

"From Mr. Youngquist," corrected Rev. Lacklund.

"Could it be he still has it on him," asked Father Dunphy, "in a money belt?"

"Impossible," Horne said. "I would have felt it when I hit him. I would have spotted it bulging under his shirt. No money belt."

"How could he possibly spend that much coming down?" asked Rev. Hollings.

Horne started to answer when a knock at the door interrupted. It opened to reveal a small man wearing a derby, a cowboy outfit, a star, and a grouchy expression.

"Marshal . . ." began Horne.

"E. A. Atwood. I don't want to know your name, I don't see a blasted thing on that bed, I don't want to hear about the fight, what started it, nothing. Don't bother to introduce me. I just came up to tell you you'd better get out of Waco. Allison's got friends here and they might not take kindly to you nearly beating him to death. There's a seven-o'clock stage heading north for Wichita Falls tomorrow morning and one coming through heading south for San Antone twenty minutes after. Take your choice, but be on one if you know what's good for you. Gentlemen . . ."

He started to close the door. Horne stopped him. He got out the ticket given him by the man who had relieved him of his weapons at the Broken Spur.

"I'd like to pick up my guns."

"Give me the stub, I'll pick them up for you. They'll be at the stage depot before seven tomorrow."

"Thanks."

The marshal fixed him with a grim look. "You sure came down heavy on old Clay. What a battering . . ."

"He stole a great deal of money," said Rev. Miller. "He's a wanted man."

"Not in Waco he's not."

With this Atwood closed the door. Horne shrugged. "Not if Marshal E.A. Atwood wants to keep breathing he's not. Ninety dollars, I don't believe it. And you, all of you, how in the world . . .?"

Father Dunphy smiled. "Did we get all the way down here? Simple, Cletus showed you his telegram from Mr. Sturdivant, the organ salesman. You went flying back to Deadwood, he told us about it, and we decided to check up on your associate."

Rev. Miller nodded. "To be honest I was very worried, Mr. Sturdivant's wire did sound so ominous. No matter what the bish—Mr. Youngquist did, restitution was made, he was penitent, he is a fellow Christian. If, heaven forbid, Allison had killed him, we all would have been very shocked and saddened."

"We rode up to Deadwood to see him," said Rev. Grier. "You'd left by the time we got there. We found him in a bad way, but happily over the danger hump. He was very worried about you. We decided to follow you, knowing your destination would be Tioga."

"But why?"

"You'd returned the money," Rev. Hollings said, "ahem, repaying the debt of your iniquity, so to speak. Knowing who you were going up against down here, we too were worried."

"We wanted to help in any way we could," said Rev. Lacklund. "The livery stable manager in Tioga said you'd taken the stage. We took the same route."

"It's amazing," Horne said.

"What's amazing about it?" asked Rev. Miller.

"Not your coming down, not that I don't appreciate it, I do. I mean, the fight. I don't know how to fight, I've never won a fight in my life; the best I've ever done is get through without being killed. My problem is basically I'm a coward with my fists. I close my eyes, duck, I can't hit the broad side of a cow. I can't break a pasteboard box, and yet I very nearly killed him."

"You were inspired," said Rev. Miller.

Rev. Lacklund nodded. "Your strength was as the strength of ten."

"Not because my heart was pure . . ."

"Because he nearly killed your friend. If there'd been five of him, you'd have beaten them all, you were so outraged."

"Feel better now?" asked Father Dunphy.

"Much. Tons. I ache all over and probably will for a month, but I feel wonderful. And you know something? I'm glad I couldn't pull the trigger."

"That," said Rev. Miller, "is highly significant. It's what distinguishes you from him."

"Amen," said Rev. Hollings.

"Amen," said Father Dunphy, Rev. Lacklund, and Rev. Grier.

"Amen," said Horne.

24

"Ninety dollars!" rasped Perry. "Ninety? Nine-oh?"

They stood outside Dr. Blue's office-infirmary, Perry supporting himself with two canes. He now could stand if unsteadily and with pain. Moving increased his discomfort, and although he'd been formally discharged as a patient, it was with the understanding that he return twice every day to be examined until further notice.

"I don't know what happened to it," Horne replied.

"Obviously you don't. Did you go back and search him?"

"He didn't have it on him, no money belt, nothing in his pockets. There was no way he could carry that much without my seeing it."

"How could you? You fought with your eyes closed. You always fight with your eyes closed."

"Not this time."

Perry grunted. "Get a stogie out of my inside pocket and light it for me."

Horne obliged him and lit a cheroot for himself.

"Did you go back and check him out the next morning? Talk to him?"

"The marshal told me he was still out cold when we left."

"You came back with Reverend Miller and the others."

"The six of us. We took the stage up to Wichita Falls and from there to Stratford. We took trains back up. We parted company in Hot Springs. They headed back to Moorcroft, then home. Perry . . ."

"What?"

"Forget about the money, it's not important."

Perry looked stunned. "Not—"

"It's not! What is it but filthy lucre? For the love of money is the root of all evil: which while some coveted after, they have erred from the faith, and pierced themselves through with many sorrows."

"What?"

"I said for the love . . ."

"I know what you said. What's the matter with you?"

"Not a thing, not anymore. Only there's something you should know: I'm a changed man. I mean it, Perry, you see before you the new T. G. Horne."

"I see before me a blithering nincompoop!"

"I'm serious. I'll never turn another card, never again will this hand hold dice, never again will the word bet cross my lips. I've seen the light. I never dreamed it could shine so brightly."

"You're running a fever."

"I'm perfectly well, my mind is clear as a bell, I know exactly what I'm saying, and I've never been more serious about anything in my entire life!"

"You're another; you just spent a whole week in the company of five sky pilots to the exclusion of the rest of all humanity. They talked to you and you listened. They've mesmerized you; they've filled you up to the eyeballs with preachification, sermonology, and holy harangue."

"They most certainly did not! All they did was talk among themselves. All I did was listen. By the time we got to Hot Springs, I felt like I was reborn. By the time I got here, I was convinced of it."

"You're making me sick to my stomach."

"I'd rather make you see the light, Uncle Pericles. You too can change your ways. You're never too old to."

The door behind them opened. Out came Dr. Blue.

"Gentlemen, lovely day, isn' it?"

"Beautiful," Horne said.

"It's all right," Perry said.

"I'm on my way to church," said the doctor. "You're both welcome to join me."

"I'd be delighted to," said Horne. "What about you, Bishop?"

Perry glared and waved them away with one cane. Horne and the doctor started off. They were nearing the corner when Perry called after them.

"Hey, wait for me. Hey!" They stopped and turned. "The legs of the lame are not equal, you know, Proverbs, Twenty-six, Verse Seven."

"So is a parable in the mouth of a fool," said Horne. "Proverbs Twenty-six, Verse Seven."

Dr. Blue laughed, Horne leered, Perry scowled and came hobbling after them.

Author's note

Clay Allison recovered from the beating. In time, wearying of a life of crime. he acquired his own ranch in Colfax County, New Mexico. On July 1, 1887, he was hauling a load of supplies home from Pecos, Texas, when a sack of grain fell off the pile; he tried to grab it and fell from the wagon. One of the wheels rolled across his neck, breaking it and killing him.

He was thirty-seven.